# THE POWER OF DARKNESS

## LEO TOLSTOY

*translated by*
**LOUISE MAUDE AND AYLMER MAUDE**

copyright © 2023 Culturea
text and cover : © public domain
Contact : infos@culturea.fr
Print in Germany by Books on Demand
Design : Derek Murphy
Layout : Reedsy (https://reedsy.com/)
ISBN : 979-10-418-0619-5
Legal deposit : June 2023
All rights reserved

# Dramatis Personae

*Peter Ignátitch. A well-to-do peasant, forty-two years old, married for the second time, and sickly*

*Anísya. His wife, thirty-two years old, fond of dress*

*Akoulína. Peter's daughter by his first marriage, sixteen years old, hard of hearing, mentally undeveloped*

*Nan (Anna Petróvna). His daughter by his second marriage, ten years old*

*Nikíta. Their labourer, twenty-five years old, fond of dress*

*Akím. Nikíta's father, fifty years old, a plain-looking, God-fearing peasant*

*Matryóna. His wife and Nikíta's mother, fifty years old*

*Marína. An orphan girl, twenty-two years old*

*Martha. Peter's sister*

*Mítritch. An old labourer, ex-soldier*

*Simon. Marína's husband*

*Bridegroom. Engaged to Akoulína*

*Iván. His father*

*A neighbour*

*First girl*

*Second girl*

*Police officer*

*Driver*

*Best man*

*Matchmaker*

*Village elder*

*Visitors, women, girls, and people come to see the wedding*

N.B.—The "oven" mentioned is the usual large, brick, Russian baking-oven. The top of it outside is flat, so that more than one person can lie on it.

# The Power of Darkness

Or, If a Claw Is Caught the Bird Is Lost

# Act I

The Act takes place in autumn in a large village. The Scene represents PETER's roomy hut. PETER is sitting on a wooden bench, mending a horse-collar. ANÍSYA and AKOULÍNA are spinning, and singing a part-song.

PETER (*Looking out of the window.*) The horses have got loose again. If we don't look out they'll be killing the colt. Nikíta! Hey, Nikíta! Is the fellow deaf? (*Listens. To the women.*) Shut up, one can't hear anything.

NIKÍTA (*From outside.*) What?

PETER Drive the horses in.

NIKÍTA We'll drive 'em in. All in good time.

PETER (*Shaking his head.*) Ah, these labourers! If I were well, I'd not keep one on no account. There's nothing but bother with 'em. (*Rises and sits down again.*) Nikíta!... It's no good shouting. One of you'd better go. Go, Akoúl, drive 'em in.

AKOULÍNA What? The horses?

PETER What else?

AKOULÍNA All right. (*Exit.*)

PETER Ah, but he's a loafer, that lad... no good at all. Won't stir a finger if he can help it.

ANÍSYA You're so mighty brisk yourself. When you're not sprawling on the top of the oven you're

|           |                                                                                                                                                     |
|-----------|-----------------------------------------------------------------------------------------------------------------------------------------------------|
|           | squatting on the bench. To goad others to work is all you're fit for.                                                                               |
| PETER     | If one weren't to goad you on a bit, one'd have no roof left over one's head before the year's out. Oh what people!                                 |
| ANÍSYA    | You go shoving a dozen jobs on to one's shoulders, and then do nothing but scold. It's easy to lie on the oven and give orders.                     |
| PETER     | (*Sighing.*) Oh, if 'twere not for this sickness that's got hold of me, I'd not keep him on another day.                                            |
| AKOULÍNA  | (*Off the scene.*) Gee up, gee, woo. (*A colt neighs, the stamping of horses' feet and the creaking of the gate are heard.*)                        |
| PETER     | Bragging, that's what he's good at. I'd like to sack him, I would indeed.                                                                           |
| ANÍSYA    | (*Mimicking him.*) "Like to sack him." You buckle to yourself, and then talk.                                                                       |
| AKOULÍNA  | (*Enters.*) It's all I could do to drive 'em in. That piebald always will…                                                                          |
| PETER     | And where's Nikíta?                                                                                                                                 |
| AKOULÍNA  | Where's Nikíta? Why, standing out there in the street.                                                                                              |
| PETER     | What's he standing there for?                                                                                                                       |
| AKOULÍNA  | What's he standing there for? He stands there jabbering.                                                                                            |
| PETER     | One can't get any sense out of her! Who's he jabbering with?                                                                                        |

AKOULÍNA (*Does not hear.*) Eh, what?

(PETER *waves her off. She sits down to her spinning.*)

NAN (*Running in to her mother.*) Nikíta's father and mother have come. They're going to take him away. It's true!

ANÍSYA Nonsense!

NAN Yes. Blest if they're not! (*Laughing.*) I was just going by, and Nikíta, he says, "Goodbye, Anna Petróvna," he says, "you must come and dance at my wedding. I'm leaving you," he says, and laughs.

ANÍSYA (*To her husband.*) There now. Much he cares. You see, he wants to leave of himself. "Sack him" indeed!

PETER Well, let him go. Just as if I couldn't find somebody else.

ANÍSYA And what about the money he's had in advance?

(NAN *stands listening at the door for awhile, and then exit.*)

PETER (*Frowning.*) The money? Well, he can work it off in summer, anyhow.

ANÍSYA Well, of course you'll be glad if he goes and you've not got to feed him. It's only me as'll have to work like a horse all the winter. That lass of yours isn't over fond of work either. And you'll be lying up on the oven. I know you.

PETER — What's the good of wearing out one's tongue before one has the hang of the matter?

ANÍSYA — The yard's full of cattle. You've not sold the cow, and have kept all the sheep for the winter: feeding and watering 'em alone takes all one's time, and you want to sack the labourer. But I tell you straight, I'm not going to do a man's work! I'll go and lie on the top of the oven same as you, and let everything go to pot! You may do what you like.

PETER — (*To* AKOULÍNA.) Go and see about the feeding, will you? it's time.

AKOULÍNA — The feeding? All right. (*Puts on a coat and takes a rope.*)

ANÍSYA — I'm not going to work for you. You go and work yourself. I've had enough of it, so there!

PETER — That'll do. What are you raving about? Like a sheep with the staggers!

ANÍSYA — You're a crazy cur, you are! One gets neither work nor pleasure from you. Eating your fill, that's all you do, you palsied cur, you!

PETER — (*Spits and puts on coat.*) Faugh! The Lord have mercy! I'd better go myself and see what's up. (*Exit.*)

ANÍSYA — (*After him.*) Scurvy long-nosed devil!

AKOULÍNA — What are you swearing at dad for?

ANÍSYA — Hold your noise, you idiot!

AKOULÍNA — (*Going to the door.*) I know why you're swearing at him. You're an idiot yourself, you

|   |   |
|---|---|
| | bitch. I'm not afraid of you. |
| ANÍSYA | What do you mean? (*Jumps up and looks round for something to hit her with.*) Mind, or I'll give you one with the poker. |
| AKOULÍNA | (*Opening the door.*) Bitch! devil! that's what you are! Devil! bitch! bitch! devil! (*Runs off.*) |
| ANÍSYA | (*Ponders.*) "Come and dance at my wedding!" What new plan is this? Marry? Mind, Nikíta, if that's your intention, I'll go and... No, I can't live without him. I won't let him go. |
| NIKÍTA | (*Enters, looks round, and seeing* ANÍSYA *alone approaches quickly. In a low tone.*) Here's a go; I'm in a regular fix! That governor of mine wants to take me away—tells me I'm to come home. Says quite straight I'm to marry and live at home. |
| ANÍSYA | Well, go and marry! What's that to me? |
| NIKÍTA | Is that it? Why, here am I reckoning how best to consider matters, and just hear her! She tells me to go and marry. Why's that? (*Winking.*) Has she forgotten? |
| ANÍSYA | Yes, go and marry! What do I care? |
| NIKÍTA | What are you spitting for? Just see, she won't even let me stroke her.... What's the matter? |
| ANÍSYA | This! That you want to play me false.... If you do—why, I don't want you either. So now you know! |
| NIKÍTA | That'll do, Anísya. Do you think I'll forget you? Never while I live! I'll not play you false, that's |

flat. I've been thinking that supposing they do go and make me marry, I'd still come back to you. If only he don't make me live at home.

ANÍSYA   Much need I'll have of you, once you're married.

NIKÍTA   There's a go now. How is it possible to go against one's father's will?

ANÍSYA   Yes, I daresay, shove it all on your father. You know it's your own doing. You've long been plotting with that slut of yours, Marína. It's she has put you up to it. She didn't come here for nothing t'other day.

NIKÍTA   Marína? What's she to me? Much I care about her!... Plenty of them buzzing around.

ANÍSYA   Then what has made your father come here? It's you have told him to. You've gone and deceived me. (*Cries.*)

NIKÍTA   Anísya, do you believe in a God or not? I never so much as dreamt of it. I know nothing at all about it. I never even dreamt of it—that's flat! My old dad has got it all out of his own pate.

ANÍSYA   If you don't wish it yourself who can force you? He can't drive you like an ass.

NIKÍTA   Well, I reckon it's not possible to go against one's parent. But it's not by my wish.

ANÍSYA   Don't you budge, that's all about it!

NIKÍTA   There was a fellow wouldn't budge, and the village elder gave him such a hiding.... That's what it might come to! I've no great wish for that sort of thing. They say it touches one up....

ANÍSYA  Shut up with your nonsense. Nikíta, listen to me: if you marry that Marína I don't know what I won't do to myself.... I shall lay hands on myself! I have sinned, I have gone against the law, but I can't go back now. If you go away I'll...

NIKÍTA  Why should I go? Had I wanted to go—I should have gone long ago. There was Iván Semyónitch t'other day—offered me a place as his coachman.... Only fancy what a life that would have been! But I did not go. Because, I reckon, I am good enough for anyone. Now if you did not love me it would be a different matter.

ANÍSYA  Yes, and that's what you should remember. My old man will die one of these fine days, I'm thinking; then we could cover our sin, make it all right and lawful, and then you'll be master here.

NIKÍTA  Where's the good of making plans? What do I care? I work as hard as if I were doing it for myself. My master loves me, and his missus loves me. And if the wenches run after me, it's not my fault, that's flat.

ANÍSYA  And you'll love me?

NIKÍTA  (*Embracing her.*) There, as you have ever been in my heart...

MATRYÓNA  (*Enters, and crosses herself a long time before the* icon. NIKÍTA *and* ANÍSYA *step apart.*) What I saw I didn't perceive, what I heard I didn't hearken to. Playing with the lass, eh? Well—even a calf will play. Why shouldn't one have some fun when one's young? But your master is out in the yard a-calling you, sonnie.

NIKÍTA I only came to get the axe.

MATRYÓNA I know, sonnie, I know; them sort of axes are mostly to be found where the women are.

NIKÍTA (*Stooping to pick up axe.*) I say, mother, is it true you want me to marry? As I reckon, that's quite unnecessary. Besides, I've got no wish that way.

MATRYÓNA Eh, honey! why should you marry? Go on as you are. It's all the old man. You'd better go, sonnie, we can talk these matters over without you.

NIKÍTA It's a queer go! One moment I'm to be married, the next, not. I can't make head or tail of it. (*Exit.*)

ANÍSYA What's it all about then? Do you really wish him to get married?

MATRYÓNA Eh, why should he marry, my jewel? It's all nonsense, all my old man's drivel. "Marry, marry." But he's reckoning without his host. You know the saying, "From oats and hay, why should horses stray?" When you've enough and to spare, why look elsewhere? And so in this case. (*Winks.*) Don't I see which way the wind blows?

ANÍSYA   Where's the good of my pretending to you, Mother Matryóna? You know all about it. I have sinned. I love your son.

MATRYÓNA   Dear me, here's news! D'you think Mother Matryóna didn't know? Eh, lassie—Mother Matryóna's been ground, and ground again, ground fine! This much I can tell you, my jewel: Mother Matryóna can see through a brick wall three feet thick. I know it all, my jewel! I know what young wives need sleeping draughts for, so I've brought some along. (*Unties a knot in her handkerchief and brings out paper-packets.*) As much as is wanted, I see, and what's not wanted I neither see nor perceive! There! Mother Matryóna has also been young. I had to know a thing or two to live with my old fool. I know seventy-and-seven dodges. But I see your old man's quite seedy, quite seedy! How's one to live with such as him? Why, if you pricked him with a hayfork it wouldn't fetch blood. See if you don't bury him before the spring. Then you'll need someone in the house. Well, what's wrong with my son? He'll do as well as another. Then where's the advantage of my taking him away from a good place? Am I my child's enemy?

ANÍSYA   Oh, if only he does not go away.

MATRYÓNA   He won't go away, birdie. It's all nonsense. You know my old man. His wits are always woolgathering; yet sometimes he takes a thing

|  |  |
|---|---|
|  | into his pate, and it's as if it were wedged in, you can't knock it out with a hammer. |
| ANÍSYA | And what started this business? |
| MATRYÓNA | Well, you see, my jewel, you yourself know what a fellow with women the lad is—and he's handsome too, though I say it as shouldn't. Well, you know, he was living at the railway, and they had an orphan wench there to cook for them. Well, that same wench took to running after him. |
| ANÍSYA | Marína? |
| MATRYÓNA | Yes, the plague seize her! Whether anything happened or not, anyhow something got to my old man's ears. Maybe he heard from the neighbours, maybe she's been and blabbed... |
| ANÍSYA | Well, she is a bold hussy! |
| MATRYÓNA | So my old man—the old blockhead—off he goes: "Marry, marry," he says, "he must marry her and cover the sin," he says. "We must take the lad home," he says, "and he shall marry," he says. Well, I did my best to make him change his mind, but, dear me, no. So, all right, thinks I—I'll try another dodge. One always has to entice them fools in this way, just pretend to be of their mind, and when it comes to the point one goes and turns it all one's own way. You know, a woman has time to think seventy-and-seven thoughts while falling off the oven, so how's such as he to see through it? "Well, yes," says I, "it would be a good job—only we must |

consider well beforehand. Why not go and see our son, and talk it over with Peter Ignátitch and hear what he has to say?" So here we are.

ANÍSYA. Oh dear, oh dear, how will it all end? Supposing his father just orders him to marry her?

MATRYÓNA. Orders, indeed. Chuck his orders to the dogs! Don't you worry; that affair will never come off. I'll go to your old man myself, and sift and strain this matter clear—there will be none of it left. I have come here only for the look of the thing. A very likely thing! Here's my son living in happiness and expecting happiness, and I'll go and match him with a slut! No fear, I'm not a fool!

ANÍSYA. And she—this Marína—came dangling after him here! Mother, would you believe, when they said he was going to marry, it was as if a knife had gone right through my heart. I thought he cared for her.

MATRYÓNA. Oh, my jewel! Why, you don't think him such a fool, that he should go and care for a homeless baggage like that? Nikíta is a sensible fellow, you see. He knows whom to love. So don't you go and fret, my jewel. We'll not take him away, and we won't marry him. No, we'll let him stay on, if you'll only oblige us with a little money.

ANÍSYA. All I know is, that I could not live if Nikíta went away.

MATRYÓNA. Naturally, when one's young it's no easy

matter! You, a wench in full bloom, to be living with the dregs of a man like that husband of yours.

ANÍSYA  Mother Matryóna, would you believe it? I'm that sick of him, that sick of this long-nosed cur of mine, I can hardly bear to look at him.

MATRYÓNA  Yes, I see, it's one of them cases. Just look here, (*looks round and whispers*) I've been to see that old man, you know—he's given me simples of two kinds. This, you see, is a sleeping draught. "Just give him one of these powders," he says, "and he'll sleep so sound you might jump on him!" And this here, "This is that kind of simple," he says, "that if you give one some of it to drink it has no smell whatever, but its strength is very great. There are seven doses here, a pinch at a time. Give him seven pinches," he says, "and she won't have far to look for freedom," he says.

ANÍSYA  O-o-oh! What's that?

MATRYÓNA  "No sign whatever," he says. He's taken a rouble for it. "Can't sell it for less," he says. Because it's no easy matter to get 'em, you know. I paid him, dearie, out of my own money. If she takes them, thinks I, it's all right; if she don't, I can let old Michael's daughter have them.

ANÍSYA  O-o-oh! But mayn't some evil come of them? I'm frightened!

MATRYÓNA  What evil, my jewel? If your old man was hale

and hearty, 'twould be a different matter, but he's neither alive nor dead as it is. He's not for this world. Such things often happen.

ANÍSYA  O-o-oh, my poor head! I'm afeared, Mother Matryóna, lest some evil come of them. No. That won't do.

MATRYÓNA  Just as you like. I might even return them to him.

ANÍSYA  And are they to be used in the same way as the others? Mixed in water?

MATRYÓNA  Better in tea, he says. "You can't notice anything," he says, "no smell nor nothing." He's a cute old fellow too.

ANÍSYA  (*Taking the powder.*) O-oh, my poor head! Could I have ever thought of such a thing if my life were not a very hell?

MATRYÓNA  You'll not forget that rouble? I promised to take it to the old man. He's had some trouble, too.

ANÍSYA  Of course? (*Goes to her box and hides the powders.*)

MATRYÓNA  And now, my jewel, keep it as close as you can, so that no one should find it out. Heaven defend that it should happen, but *if* anyone notices it, tell 'em it's for the black-beetles. (*Takes the rouble.*) It's also used for beetles. (*Stops short.*)

(*Enter* AKÍM, *who crosses himself in front of the icon, and then* PETER, *who sits down.*)

PETER  Well then, how's it to be, Daddy Akím?

AKÍM   As it's best, Peter Ignátitch, as it's best... I mean—as it's best. 'Cos why? I'm afeared of what d'you call 'ems, some tomfoolery, you know. I'd like to, what d'you call it... to start, you know, start the lad honest, I mean. But supposing you'd rather, what d'you call it, we might, I mean, what's name? As it's best...

PETER   All right. All right. Sit down and let's talk it over. (AKÍM *sits down*.) Well then, what's it all about? You want him to marry?

MATRYÓNA   As to marrying, he might bide a while, Peter Ignátitch. You know our poverty, Peter Ignátitch. What's he to marry on? We've hardly enough to eat ourselves. How can he marry then?...

PETER   You must consider what will be best.

MATRYÓNA   Where's the hurry for him to get married? Marriage is not that sort of thing, it's not like ripe raspberries that drop off if not picked in time.

PETER   If he were to get married, 'twould be a good thing in a way.

AKÍM   We'd like to... what d'you call it? 'Cos why, you see. I've what d'you call it... a job. I mean, I've found a paying job in town, you know.

MATRYÓNA   And a fine job too—cleaning out cesspools. The other day when he came home, I could do nothing but spew and spew. Faugh!

AKÍM   It's true, at first it does seem what d'you call

it... knocks one clean over, you know—the smell, I mean. But one gets used to it, and then it's nothing, no worse than malt grain, and then it's, what d'you call it,... pays, pays, I mean. And as to the smell being, what d'you call it, it's not for the likes of us to complain. And one changes one's clothes. So we'd like to take what's his name... Nikíta I mean, home. Let him manage things at home while I, what d'you call it—earn something in town.

PETER  You want to keep your son at home? Yes, that would be well: but how about the money he has had in advance?

AKÍM  That's it, that's it! It's just as you say, Ignátitch, it's just what d'you call it. 'Cos why? If you go into service, it's as good as if you had sold yourself, they say. That will be all right. I mean he may stay and serve his time, only he must, what d'you call it, get married. I mean—so: you let him off for a little while, that he may, what d'you call it?

PETER  Yes, we could manage that.

MATRYÓNA  Ah, but it's not yet settled between ourselves, Peter Ignátitch. I'll speak to you as I would before God, and you may judge between my old man and me. He goes on harping on that marriage. But just ask—who it is he wants him to marry. If it were a girl of the right sort now—I am not my child's enemy, but the wench is not honest.

AKÍM      No, that's wrong! Wrong, I say. 'Cos why? She, that same girl—it's my son as has offended, offended the girl I mean.

PETER     How offended?

AKÍM      That's how. She's what d'you call it, with him, with my son, Nikíta. With Nikíta, what d'you call it, I mean.

MATRYÓNA  You wait a bit, my tongue runs smoother—let me tell it. You know, this lad of ours lived at the railway before he came to you. There was a girl there as kept dangling after him. A girl of no account, you know, her name's Marína. She used to cook for the men. So now this same girl accuses our son, Nikíta, that he, so to say, deceived her.

PETER     Well, there's nothing good in that.

MATRYÓNA  But she's no honest girl herself; she runs after the fellows like a common slut.

AKÍM      There you are again, old woman, and it's not at all what d'you call it, it's all not what d'you call it, I mean...

MATRYÓNA  There now, that's all the sense one gets from my old owl—"what d'you call it, what d'you call it," and he doesn't know himself what he means. Peter Ignátitch, don't listen to me, but go yourself and ask anyone you like about the girl, everybody will say the same. She's just a homeless good-for-nothing.

PETER     You know, Daddy Akím, if that's how things

|||||||||are, there's no reason for him to marry her. A daughter-in-law's not like a shoe, you can't kick her off.

AKÍM — (*Excitedly.*) It's false, old woman, it's what d'you call it, false; I mean, about the girl; false! 'Cos why? The lass is a good lass, a very good lass, you know. I'm sorry, sorry for the lassie, I mean.

MATRYÓNA — It's an old saying: "For the wide world old Miriam grieves, and at home without bread her children she leaves." He's sorry for the girl, but not sorry for his own son! Sling her round your neck and carry her about with you! That's enough of such empty cackle!

AKÍM — No, it's not empty.

MATRYÓNA — There, don't interrupt, let me have my say.

AKÍM — (*Interrupts.*) No, not empty! I mean, you twist things your own way, about the lass or about yourself. Twist them, I mean, to make it better for yourself; but God, what d'you call it, turns them His way. That's how it is.

MATRYÓNA — Eh! One only wears out one's tongue with you.

AKÍM — The lass is hardworking and spruce, and keeps everything round herself... what d'you call it. And in our poverty, you know, it's a pair of hands, I mean; and the wedding needn't cost much. But the chief thing's the offence, the offence to the lass, and she's a what d'you call it, an orphan, you know; that's what she is, and there's the offence.

MATRYÓNA  Eh! they'll all tell you a tale of that sort...

ANÍSYA  Daddy Akím, you'd better listen to us women; we can tell you a thing or two.

AKÍM  And God, how about God? Isn't she a human being, the lass? A what d'you call it—also a human being I mean, before God. And how do you look at it?

MATRYÓNA  Eh!... started off again?...

PETER  Wait a bit, Daddy Akím. One can't believe all these girls say, either. The lad's alive, and not far away; send for him, and find out straight from him if it's true. He won't wish to lose his soul. Go and call the fellow, (ANÍSYA *rises*) and tell him his father wants him. (*Exit* ANÍSYA.)

MATRYÓNA  That's right, dear friend; you've cleared the way clean, as with water. Yes, let the lad speak for himself. Nowadays, you know, they'll not let you force a son to marry; one must first of all ask the lad. He'll never consent to marry her and disgrace himself, not for all the world. To my thinking, it's best he should go on living with you and serving you as his master. And we need not take him home for the summer either; we can hire a help. If you would only give us ten roubles now, we'll let him stay on.

PETER  All in good time. First let us settle one thing before we start another.

AKÍM  You see, Peter Ignátitch, I speak. 'Cos why? you know how it happens. We try to fix things up as seems best for ourselves, you know; and as to God, we what d'you call it, we forget Him. We think it's best so, turn it our own way, and lo! we've got into a fix, you know. We think it will be best, I mean; and lo! it turns out much worse—without God, I mean.

PETER  Of course one must not forget God.

AKÍM  It turns out worse! But when it's the right way—God's way—it what d'you call it, it gives one joy; seems pleasant, I mean. So I reckon, you see, get him, the lad, I mean, get him to marry her, to keep him from sin, I mean, and let him what d'you call it at home, as it's lawful, I mean, while I go and get the job in town. The work is of the right sort—it's payin', I mean. And in God's sight it's what d'you call it—it's best, I mean. Ain't she an orphan? Here, for example, a year ago some fellows went and took timber from the steward—thought they'd do the steward, you know. Yes, they did the steward, but they couldn't what d'you call it—do God, I mean. Well, and so...

(*Enter* NIKÍTA *and* NAN.)

NIKÍTA  You called me? (*Sits down and takes out his tobacco-pouch.*)

PETER  (*In a low, reproachful voice.*) What are you thinking about—have you no manners? Your father is going to speak to you, and you sit down and fool about with tobacco. Come, get up!

(NIKÍTA *rises, leans carelessly with his elbow on the table, and smiles.*)

AKÍM  It seems there's a complaint, you know, about you, Nikíta—a complaint, I mean, a complaint.

NIKÍTA  Who's been complaining?

AKÍM  Complaining? It's a maid, an orphan maid, complaining, I mean. It's her, you know—a complaint against you, from Marína, I mean.

NIKÍTA  (*Laughs.*) Well, that's a good one. What's the complaint? And who's told you—she herself?

AKÍM  It's I am asking you, and you must now, what d'you call it, give me an answer. Have you got mixed up with the lass, I mean—mixed up, you know?

NIKÍTA  I don't know what you mean. What's up?

AKÍM  Foolin', I mean, what d'you call it? foolin'. Have you been foolin' with her, I mean?

NIKÍTA  Never mind what's been! Of course one does have some fun with a cook now and then to while away the time. One plays the concertina and gets her to dance. What of that?

PETER  Don't shuffle, Nikíta, but answer your father straight out.

AKÍM  (*Solemnly.*) You can hide it from men but not from God, Nikíta. You, what d'you call it—think, I mean, and don't tell lies. She's an orphan; so, you see, anyone is free to insult her. An orphan, you see. So you should say what's rightest.

NIKÍTA   But what if I have nothing to say? I have told you everything—because there isn't anything to tell, that's flat! (*Getting excited.*) She can go and say anything about me, same as if she was speaking of one as is dead. Why don't she say anything about Fédka Mikíshin? Besides, how's this, that one mayn't even have a bit of fun nowadays? And as for her, well, she's free to say anything she likes.

AKÍM   Ah, Nikíta, mind! A lie will out. Did anything happen?

NIKÍTA   (*Aside.*) How he sticks to it; it's too bad. (*To* AKÍM.) I tell you, I know nothing more. There's been nothing between us. (*Angrily.*) By God! and may I never leave this spot (*crosses himself*) if I know anything about it. (*Silence. Then still more excitedly.*) Why! have you been thinking of getting me to marry her? What do you mean by it?—it's a confounded shame. Besides, nowadays you've got no such rights as to force a fellow to marry. That's plain enough. Besides, haven't I sworn I know nothing about it?

MATRYÓNA   (*To her husband.*) There now, that's just like your silly pate, to believe all they tell you. He's gone and put the lad to shame all for nothing. The best thing is to let him live as he is living, with his master. His master will help us in our present need, and give us ten roubles, and when the time comes…

PETER   Well, Daddy Akím, how's it to be?

AKÍM    (*Looks at his son, clicking his tongue disapprovingly.*) Mind, Nikíta, the tears of one that's been wronged never, what d'you call it—never fall beside the mark but always on, what's name—the head of the man as did the wrong. So mind, don't what d'you call it.

NIKÍTA    (*Sits down.*) What's there to mind? mind yourself.

NAN    (*Aside.*) I must run and tell mother. (*Exit.*)

MATRYÓNA    (*To* PETER.) That's always the way with this old mumbler of mine, Peter Ignátitch. Once he's got anything wedged in his pate there's no knocking it out. We've gone and troubled you all for nothing. The lad can go on living as he has been. Keep him; he's your servant.

PETER    Well, Daddy Akím, what do you say?

AKÍM    Why, the lad's his own master, if only he what d'you call it…. I only wish that, what d'you call it, I mean.

MATRYÓNA    You don't know yourself what you're jawing about. The lad himself has no wish to leave. Besides, what do we want with him at home? We can manage without him.

PETER    Only one thing, Daddy Akím—if you are thinking of taking him back in summer, I don't want him here for the winter. If he is to stay at all, it must be for the whole year.

MATRYÓNA    And it's for a year he'll bind himself. If we want help when the press of work comes, we can hire help, and the lad shall remain with you. Only give us ten roubles now....

PETER  Well then, is it to be for another year?

AKÍM  (*Sighing.*) Yes, it seems, it what d'you call it... if it's so, I mean, it seems that it must be what d'you call it.

MATRYÓNA  For a year, counting from St. Dimítry's day. We know you'll pay him fair wages. But give us ten roubles now. Help us out of our difficulties. (*Gets up and bows to* PETER.)

(*Enter* NAN *and* ANÍSYA. *The latter sits down at one side.*)

PETER  Well, if that's settled we might step across to the inn and have a drink. Come, Daddy Akím, what do you say to a glass of vódka?

AKÍM  No, I never drink that sort of thing.

PETER  Well, you'll have some tea?

AKÍM  Ah, tea! yes, I do sin that way. Yes, tea's the thing.

PETER  And the women will also have some tea. Come. And you, Nikíta, go and drive the sheep in and clear away the straw.

NIKÍTA  All right. (*Exeunt all but* NIKÍTA. NIKÍTA *lights a cigarette. It grows darker.*) Just see how they bother one. Want a fellow to tell 'em how he larks about with the wenches! It would take long to tell 'em all those stories—"Marry her," he says. Marry them all! One would have a good lot of wives! And what need have I to marry? Am as good as married now! There's many a chap as envies me. Yet how strange it felt when I crossed myself before the icon. It was just as if someone shoved me. The whole web fell to pieces at once. They say it's frightening to swear what's not true. That's all humbug. It's all talk, that is. It's simple enough.

AKOULÍNA (*Enters with a rope, which she puts down. She takes off her outdoor things and goes into closet.*) You might at least have got a light.

NIKÍTA What, to look at you? I can see you well enough without.

AKOULÍNA Oh, bother you!

(NAN *enters and whispers to* NIKÍTA.)

NAN Nikíta, there's a person wants you. There is!

NIKÍTA What person?

NAN Marína from the railway; she's out there, round the corner.

NIKÍTA Nonsense!

NAN Blest if she isn't!

NIKÍTA What does she want?

NAN She wants you to come out. She says, "I only want to say a word to Nikíta." I began asking, but she won't tell, but only says, "Is it true he's leaving you?" And I say, "No, only his father wanted to take him away and get him to marry, but he won't, and is going to stay with us another year." And she says, "For goodness' sake send him out to me. I must see him," she says, "I must say a word to him somehow." She's been waiting a long time. Why don't you go?

NIKÍTA  Bother her! What should I go for?

NAN  She says, "If he don't come, I'll go into the hut to him." Blest if she didn't say she'd come in!

NIKÍTA  Not likely. She'll wait a bit and then go away.

NAN  "Or is it," she says, "that they want him to marry Akoulína?"

(*Re-enter* AKOULÍNA, *passing near* NIKÍTA *to take her distaff.*)

AKOULÍNA  Marry whom to Akoulína?

NAN  Why, Nikíta.

AKOULÍNA  A likely thing! Who says it?

NIKÍTA  (*Looks at her and laughs.*) It seems people do say it. Would you marry me, Akoulína?

AKOULÍNA  Who, you? Perhaps I might have afore, but I won't now.

NIKÍTA  And why not now?

AKOULÍNA  'Cos you wouldn't love me.

NIKÍTA  Why not?

AKOULÍNA  'Cos you'd be forbidden to. (*Laughs.*)

NIKÍTA  Who'd forbid it?

AKOULÍNA  Who? My stepmother. She does nothing but grumble, and is always staring at you.

NIKÍTA  (*Laughing.*) Just hear her! Ain't she cute?

AKOULÍNA  Who? Me? What's there to be cute about? Am I blind? She's been rowing and rowing at dad all

|  |  |
|---|---|
| | day. The fat-muzzled witch! (*Goes into closet.*) |
| NAN | (*Looking out of the window.*) Look, Nikíta, she's coming! I'm blest if she isn't! I'll go away. (*Exit.*) |
| MARÍNA | (*Enters.*) What are you doing with me? |
| NIKÍTA | Doing? I'm not doing anything. |
| MARÍNA | You mean to desert me. |
| NIKÍTA | (*Gets up angrily.*) What does this look like, your coming here? |
| MARÍNA | Oh, Nikíta! |
| NIKÍTA | Well, you are strange! What have you come for? |
| MARÍNA | Nikíta! |
| NIKÍTA | That's my name. What do you want with Nikíta? Well, what next? Go away, I tell you! |
| MARÍNA | I see, you do want to throw me over. |
| NIKÍTA | Well, and what's there to remember? You yourself don't know. When you stood out there round the corner and sent Nan for me, and I didn't come, wasn't it plain enough that you're not wanted? It seems pretty simple. So there—go! |
| MARÍNA | Not wanted! So now I'm not wanted! I believed you when you said you would love me. And now that you've ruined me, I'm not wanted. |
| NIKÍTA | Where's the good of talking? This is quite improper. You've been telling tales to father. Now, do go away, will you? |

MARÍNA   You know yourself I never loved anyone but you. Whether you married me or not, I'd not have been angry. I've done you no wrong, then why have you left off caring for me? Why?

NIKÍTA   Where's the use of baying at the moon? You go away. Goodness me! what a duffer!

MARÍNA   It's not that you deceived me when you promised to marry me that hurts, but that you've left off loving. No, it's not that you've stopped loving me either, but that you've changed me for another, that's what hurts. I know who it is!

NIKÍTA   (*Comes up to her viciously.*) Eh! what's the good of talking to the likes of you, that won't listen to reason? Be off, or you'll drive me to do something you'll be sorry for.

MARÍNA   What, will you strike me, then? Well then, strike me! What are you turning away for? Ah, Nikíta!

NIKÍTA   Supposing someone came in. Of course, it's quite improper. And what's the good of talking?

MARÍNA   So this is the end of it! What has been has flown. You want me to forget it? Well then, Nikíta, listen. I kept my maiden honour as the apple of my eye. You have ruined me for nothing, you have deceived me. You have no pity on a fatherless and motherless girl! (*Weeping.*) You have deserted, you have killed me, but I bear you no malice. God forgive you!

If you find a better one you'll forget me, if a worse one you'll remember me. Yes, you will remember, Nikíta! Goodbye, then, if it is to be. Oh, how I loved you! Goodbye for the last time. (*Takes his head in her hands and tries to kiss him.*)

NIKÍTA  (*Tossing his head back.*) I'm not going to talk with the likes of you. If you won't go away I will, and you may stay here by yourself.

MARÍNA  (*Screams.*) You are a brute. (*In the doorway.*) God will give you no joy. (*Exit, crying.*)

AKOULÍNA  (*Comes out of closet.*) You're a dog, Nikíta!

NIKÍTA  What's up?

AKOULÍNA  What a cry she gave! (*Cries.*)

NIKÍTA  What's up with you?

AKOULÍNA  What's up? You've hurt her so. That's the way you'll hurt me also. You're a dog. (*Exit into closet.*)

(*Silence.*)

NIKÍTA  Here's a fine muddle. I'm as sweet as honey on the lasses, but when a fellow's sinned with 'em it's a bad lookout!

(*Curtain.*)

# Act II

*The scene represents the village street. To the left the outside of* PETER's *hut, built of logs, with a porch in the middle; to the right of the hut the gates and a corner of the yard buildings.* ANÍSYA *is beating hemp in the street near the corner of the yard. Six months have elapsed since the First Act.*

ANÍSYA (*Stops and listens.*) Mumbling something again. He's probably got off the stove.

(AKOULÍNA *enters, carrying two pails on a yoke.*)

ANÍSYA He's calling. You go and see what he wants, kicking up such a row.

AKOULÍNA Why don't you go?

ANÍSYA Go, I tell you! (*Exit* AKOULÍNA *into hut.*) He's bothering me to death. Won't let out where the money is, and that's all about it. He was out in the passage the other day. He must have been hiding it there. Now, I don't know myself where it is. Thank goodness he's afraid of parting with it, so that at least it will stay in the house. If only I could manage to find it. He hadn't it on him yesterday. Now I don't know where it can be. He has quite worn the life out of me.

(*Enter* AKOULÍNA, *tying her kerchief over her head.*)

ANÍSYA  Where are you off to?

AKOULÍNA  Where? Why, he's told me to go for Aunt Martha. "Fetch my sister," he says. "I am going to die," he says. "I have a word to say to her."

ANÍSYA  (*Aside.*) Asking for his sister? Oh my poor head! Sure he wants to give it her. What shall I do? Oh! (*To* AKOULÍNA.) Don't go! Where are you off to?

AKOULÍNA  To call Aunt.

ANÍSYA  Don't go I tell you, I'll go myself. You go and take the clothes to the river to rinse. Else you'll not have finished by the evening.

AKOULÍNA  But he told me to go.

ANÍSYA  You go and do as you're bid. I tell you I'll fetch Martha myself. Take the shirts off the fence.

AKOULÍNA  The shirts? But maybe you'll not go. He's given the order.

ANÍSYA  Didn't I say I'd go? Where's Nan?

AKOULÍNA  Nan? Minding the calves.

ANÍSYA  Send her here. I dare say they'll not run away. (AKOULÍNA *collects the clothes, and exit.*)

ANÍSYA  If one doesn't go he'll scold. If one goes he'll give the money to his sister. All my trouble will be wasted. I don't myself know what I'm to do. My poor head's splitting. (*Continues to work.*)

(*Enter* MATRYÓNA, *with a stick and a bundle, in outdoor clothes.*)

MATRYÓNA   May the Lord help you, honey.

ANÍSYA   (*Looks round, stops working, and claps her hands with joy.*) Well, I never expected this! Mother Matryóna, God has sent the right guest at the right time.

MATRYÓNA   Well, how are things?

ANÍSYA   Ah, I'm driven well-nigh crazy. It's awful!

MATRYÓNA   Well, still alive, I hear?

ANÍSYA   Oh, don't talk about it. He doesn't live and doesn't die!

MATRYÓNA   But the money—has he given it to anybody?

ANÍSYA   He's just sending for his sister Martha—probably about the money.

MATRYÓNA   Well, naturally! But hasn't he given it to anyone else?

ANÍSYA   To no one. I watch like a hawk.

MATRYÓNA   And where is it?

ANÍSYA   He doesn't let out. And I can't find out in any way. He hides it now here, now there, and I can't do anything because of Akoulína. Idiot though she is, she keeps watch, and is always about. Oh my poor head! I'm bothered to death.

MATRYÓNA   Oh, my jewel, if he gives the money to anyone but you, you'll never cease regretting it as long as you live! They'll turn you out of house and home without anything. You've been worriting, and worriting all your life with one

|        |        |
|---:|:---|
| | you don't love, and will have to go a-begging when you are a widow. |
| ANÍSYA | No need to tell me, mother. My heart's that weary, and I don't know what to do. No one to get a bit of advice from. I told Nikíta, but he's frightened of the job. The only thing he did was to tell me yesterday it was hidden under the floor. |
| MATRYÓNA | Well, and did you look there? |
| ANÍSYA | I couldn't. The old man himself was in the room. I notice that sometimes he carries it about on him, and sometimes he hides it. |
| MATRYÓNA | But you, my lass, must remember that if once he gives you the slip there's no getting it right again! (*Whispering.*) Well, and did you give him the strong tea? |
| ANÍSYA | Oh! oh!... (*About to answer, but sees neighbour and stops.*) |
| | (*The neighbour (a woman) passes the hut, and listens to a call from within.*) |
| NEIGHBOUR | (*To* ANÍSYA.) I say, Anísya! Eh, Anísya! There's your old man calling, I think. |
| ANÍSYA | That's the way he always coughs—just as if he were screaming. He's getting very bad. |
| NEIGHBOUR | (*Approaches* MATRYÓNA.) How do you do, granny? Have you come far? |
| MATRYÓNA | Straight from home, dear. Come to see my son. Brought him some shirts—can't help thinking |

of these things, you see, when it's one's own child.

NEIGHBOUR  Yes, that's always so. (*To* ANÍSYA.) And I was thinking of beginning to bleach the linen, but it is a bit early, no one has begun yet.

ANÍSYA  Where's the hurry?

MATRYÓNA  Well, and has he had communion?

ANÍSYA  Oh dear yes, the priest was here yesterday.

NEIGHBOUR  I had a look at him yesterday. Dearie me! one wonders his body and soul keep together. And, O Lord, the other day he seemed just at his last gasp, so that they laid him under the holy icons.[1] They started lamenting and got ready to lay him out.

ANÍSYA  He came to, and creeps about again.

MATRYÓNA  Well, and is he to have extreme unction?

ANÍSYA  The neighbours advise it. If he lives till tomorrow we'll send for the priest.

NEIGHBOUR  Oh, Anísya dear, I should think your heart must be heavy. As the saying goes, "Not he is sick that's ill in bed, but he that sits and waits in dread."

ANÍSYA  Yes, if it were only over one way or other!

NEIGHBOUR  Yes, that's true, dying for a year, it's no joke. You're bound hand and foot like that.

MATRYÓNA  Ah, but a widow's lot is also bitter. It's all right as long as one's young, but who'll care for you when you're old? Oh yes, old age is not pleasure. Just look at me. I've not walked very far, and yet am so footsore I don't know how to stand. Where's my son?

ANÍSYA   Ploughing. But you come in and we'll get the samovar ready; the tea'll set you up again.

MATRYÓNA   (*Sitting down.*) Yes, it's true, I'm quite done up, my dears. As to extreme unction, that's absolutely necessary. Besides, they say it's good for the soul.

ANÍSYA   Yes, we'll send tomorrow.

MATRYÓNA   Yes, you had better. And we've had a wedding down in our parts.

NEIGHBOUR   What, in spring?[2]

MATRYÓNA   Ah, now if it were a poor man, then, as the saying is, it's always unseasonable for a poor man to marry. But it's Simon Matvéyitch, he's married that Marína.

ANÍSYA   What luck for her!

NEIGHBOUR   He's a widower. I suppose there are children?

MATRYÓNA   Four of 'em. What decent girl would have him! Well, so he's taken her, and she's glad. You see, the vessel was not sound, so the wine trickled out.

NEIGHBOUR   Oh my! And what do people say to it? And he, a rich peasant!

MATRYÓNA   They are living well enough so far.

NEIGHBOUR   Yes, it's true enough. Who wants to marry where there are children? There now, there's our Michael. He's such a fellow, dear me…

PEASANT'S VOICE  Hullo, Mávra. Where the devil are you? Go and drive the cow in.

(*Exit* NEIGHBOUR.)

MATRYÓNA  (*While the* NEIGHBOUR *is within hearing speaks in her ordinary voice.*) Yes, lass, thank goodness, she's married. At any rate my old fool won't go bothering about Nikíta. Now (*suddenly changing her tone*), she's gone! (*Whispers.*) I say, did you give him the tea?

ANÍSYA  Don't speak about it. He'd better die of himself. It's no use—he doesn't die, and I have only taken a sin on my soul. O-oh, my head, my head! Oh, why did you give me those powders?

MATRYÓNA  What of the powders? The sleeping powders, lass—why not give them? No evil can come of them.

ANÍSYA  I am not talking of the sleeping ones, but the others, the white ones.

MATRYÓNA  Well, honey, those powders are medicinal.

ANÍSYA  (*Sighs.*) I know, yet it's frightening. Though he's worried me to death.

MATRYÓNA  Well, and did you use many?

ANÍSYA  I gave two doses.

MATRYÓNA  Was anything noticeable?

ANÍSYA  I had a taste of the tea myself—just a little bitter. And he drank them with the tea and says, "Even tea disgusts me," and I say,

"Everything tastes bitter when one's sick." But I felt that scared, mother.

MATRYÓNA  Don't go thinking about it. The more one thinks the worse it is.

ANÍSYA  I wish you'd never given them to me and led me into sin. When I think of it something seems to tear my heart. Oh dear, why did you give them to me?

MATRYÓNA  What do you mean, honey? Lord help you! Why are you turning it on to me? Mind, lass, don't go twisting matters from the sick on to the healthy. If anything were to happen, I stand aside! I know nothing! I'm aware of nothing! I'll kiss the cross on it; I never gave you any kind of powders, never saw any, never heard of any, and never knew there were such powders. You think about yourself, lass. Why, we were talking about you the other day. "Poor thing, what torture she endures. The stepdaughter an idiot; the old man rotten, sucking her lifeblood. What wouldn't one be ready to do in such a case!"

ANÍSYA  I'm not going to deny it. A life such as mine could make one do worse than that. It could make you hang yourself or throttle him. Is this a life?

MATRYÓNA  That's just it. There's no time to stand gaping; the money must be found one way or other, and then he must have his tea.

ANÍSYA  O-oh, my head, my head! I can't think what to

do. I am so frightened; he'd better die of himself. I don't want to have it on my soul.

MATRYÓNA  (*Viciously.*) And why doesn't he show the money? Does he mean to take it along with him? Is no one to have it? Is that right? God forbid such a sum should be lost all for nothing. Isn't that a sin? What's he doing? Is he worth considering?

ANÍSYA  I don't know anything. He's worried me to death.

MATRYÓNA  What is it you don't know? The business is clear. If you make a slip now, you'll repent it all your life. He'll give the money to his sister and you'll be left without.

ANÍSYA  O-oh dear! Yes, and he did send for her—I must go.

MATRYÓNA  You wait a bit and light the samovar first. We'll give him some tea and search him together—we'll find it, no fear.

ANÍSYA  Oh dear, oh dear; supposing something were to happen.

MATRYÓNA  What now? What's the good of waiting? Do you want the money to slip from your hand when it's just in sight? You go and do as I say.

ANÍSYA  Well, I'll go and light the samovar.

MATRYÓNA  Go, honey, do the business so as not to regret it afterwards. That's right! (ANÍSYA *turns to go.* MATRYÓNA *calls her back.*)

MATRYÓNA  Just a word. Don't tell Nikíta about the

business. He's silly. God forbid he should find out about the powders. The Lord only knows what he would do. He's so tenderhearted. D'you know, he usen't to be able to kill a chicken. Don't tell him. 'Twould be a fine go, he wouldn't understand things. (*Stops horror-struck as* PETER *appears in the doorway.*)

PETER  (*Holding on to the wall, creeps out into the porch and calls with a faint voice.*) How's it one can't make you hear? Oh, oh, Anísya! Who's there? (*Drops on the bench.*)

ANÍSYA  (*Steps from behind the corner.*) Why have you come out? You should have stayed where you were lying.

PETER  Has the girl gone for Martha? It's very hard.... Oh, if only death would come quicker!

ANÍSYA  She had no time. I sent her to the river. Wait a bit, I'll go myself when I'm ready.

PETER  Send Nan. Where's she? Oh, I'm that bad! Oh, death's at hand!

ANÍSYA  I've sent for her already.

PETER  Oh dear! Then where is she?

ANÍSYA  Where's she got to, the plague seize her!

PETER  Oh, dear! I can't bear it. All my inside's on fire. It's as if a gimlet were boring me. Why have you left me as if I were a dog?... no one to give me a drink.... Oh... send Nan to me.

ANÍSYA  Here she is. Nan, go to father.

(NAN *runs in.* ANÍSYA *goes behind the corner of*

*the house.*)

PETER   Go you. Oh... to Aunt Martha, tell her father wants her; say she's to come, I want her.

NAN   All right.

PETER   Wait a bit. Tell her she's to come quick. Tell her I'm dying. O-oh!

NAN   I'll just get my shawl and be off. (*Runs off.*)

MATRYÓNA   (*Winking.*) Now then, mind and look sharp, lass. Go into the hut, hunt about everywhere, like a dog that's hunting for fleas: look under everything, and I'll search him.

ANÍSYA   (*To* MATRYÓNA.) I feel a bit bolder, somehow, now you're here. (*Goes up to porch. To* PETER.) Hadn't I better light the samovar? Here's Mother Matryóna come to see her son; you'll have a cup of tea with her?

PETER   Well then, light it. (ANÍSYA *goes into the house.* MATRYÓNA *comes up to the porch.*)

PETER   How do you do?

MATRYÓNA   (*Bowing.*) How d'you do, my benefactor; how d'you do, my precious... still ill, I see. And my old man, he's that sorry! "Go," says he, "see how he's getting on." He sends his respects to you. (*Bows again.*)

PETER   I'm dying.

MATRYÓNA   Ah yes, Peter Ignátitch, now I look at you I see, as the saying has it, "Sickness lives where men live." You've shrivelled, shrivelled, all to nothing, poor dear, now I come to look at you. Seems illness does not add to good looks.

PETER  My last hour has come.

MATRYÓNA  Oh well, Peter Ignátitch, it's God's will you know, you've had communion, and you'll have unction, God willing. Your missus is a wise woman, the Lord be thanked; she'll give you a good burial, and have prayers said for your soul, all most respectable! And my son, he'll look after things meanwhile.

PETER  There'll be no one to manage things! She's not steady. Has her head full of folly—why, I know all about it, I know. And my girl is silly and young. I've got the homestead together, and there's no one to attend to things. One can't help feeling it. (*Whimpers.*)

MATRYÓNA  Why, if it's money, or something, you can leave orders.

PETER  (*To* ANÍSYA *inside the house.*) Has Nan gone?

MATRYÓNA  (*Aside.*) There now, he's remembered!

ANÍSYA  (*From inside.*) She went then and there. Come inside, won't you? I'll help you in.

PETER  Let me sit here a bit for the last time. The air's so stuffy inside. Oh, how bad I feel! Oh, my heart's burning.... Oh, if death would only come.

MATRYÓNA  If God don't take a soul, the soul can't go out. Death and life are in God's will, Peter Ignátitch. You can't be sure of death either.

|  |  |
|---|---|
| | Maybe you'll recover yet. There was a man in our village just like that, at the very point of death... |
| PETER | No, I feel I shall die today, I feel it. (*Leans back and shuts his eyes.*) |
| ANÍSYA | (*Enters.*) Well now, are you coming in or not? You do keep one waiting. Peter! eh, Peter! |
| MATRYÓNA | (*Steps aside and beckons to* ANÍSYA *with her finger.*) Well? |
| ANÍSYA | (*Comes down the porch steps.*) Not there. |
| MATRYÓNA | But have you searched everywhere? Under the floor? |
| ANÍSYA | No, it's not there either. In the shed perhaps; he was rummaging there yesterday. |
| MATRYÓNA | Go, search, search for all you're worth. Go all over everywhere, as if you licked with your tongue! But I see he'll die this very day, his nails are turning blue and his face looks earthy. Is the samovar ready? |
| ANÍSYA | Just on the boil. |
| NIKÍTA | (*Comes from the other side, if possible on horseback, up to the gate, and does not see* PETER. *To* MATRYÓNA.) How d'you do, mother, is all well at home? |
| MATRYÓNA | The Lord be thanked, we're all alive and have a crust to bite. |
| NIKÍTA | Well, and how's master? |
| MATRYÓNA | Hush, there he sits. (*Points to porch.*) |

NIKÍTA  Well, let him sit. What's it to me?

PETER  (*Opens his eyes.*) Nikíta, I say, Nikíta, come here! (NIKÍTA *approaches.* ANÍSYA *and* MATRYÓNA *whisper together.*)

PETER  Why have you come back so early?

NIKÍTA  I've finished ploughing.

PETER  Have you done the strip beyond the bridge?

NIKÍTA  It's too far to go there.

PETER  Too far? From here it's still farther. You'll have to go on purpose now. You might have made one job of it. (ANÍSYA, *without showing herself, stands and listens.*)

MATRYÓNA  (*Approaches.*) Oh, sonnie, why don't you take more pains for your master? Your master is ill and depends on you; you should serve him as you would your own father, straining every muscle just as I always tell you to.

PETER  Well then—o-oh!... Get out the seed potatoes, and the women will go and sort them.

ANÍSYA  (*Aside.*) No fear, I'm not going. He's again sending everyone away; he must have the money on him now, and wants to hide it somewhere.

PETER  Else... o-oh! when the time comes for planting, they'll all be rotten. Oh, I can't stand it! (*Rises.*)

MATRYÓNA  (*Runs up into the porch and holds* PETER *up.*) Shall I help you into the hut?

PETER  Help me in. (*Stops.*) Nikíta!

NIKÍTA  (*Angrily.*) What now?

PETER  I shan't see you again... I'll die today.... Forgive me,³ for Christ's sake, forgive me if I have ever sinned against you... If I have sinned in word or deed... There's been all sorts of things. Forgive me!

NIKÍTA  What's there to forgive? I'm a sinner myself.

MATRYÓNA  Ah, sonnie, have some feeling.

PETER  Forgive me, for Christ's sake. (*Weeps.*)

NIKÍTA  (*Snivels.*) God will forgive you, Daddy Peter. I have no cause to complain of you. You've never done me any wrong. You forgive me; maybe I've sinned worse against you. (*Weeps.*)

(PETER *goes in whimpering,* MATRYÓNA *supporting him.*)

ANÍSYA  Oh, my poor head! It's not without some reason he's hit on that. (*Approaches* NIKÍTA.) Why did you say the money was under the floor? It's not there.

NIKÍTA  (*Does not answer, but cries.*) I have never had anything bad from him, nothing but good, and what have I gone and done!

ANÍSYA  Enough now! Where's the money?

NIKÍTA  (*Angrily.*) How should I know? Go and look for it yourself!

ANÍSYA  What's made you so tender?

NIKÍTA  I am sorry for him—that sorry. How he cried! Oh dear!

ANÍSYA  Look at him—seized with pity! He has found someone to pity too! He's been treating you like a dog, and even just now was giving orders to have you turned out of the house. You'd better show me some pity!

NIKÍTA  What are you to be pitied for?

ANÍSYA  If he dies, and the money's been hidden away…

NIKÍTA  No fear, he'll not hide it…

ANÍSYA  Oh, Nikíta darling! he's sent for his sister, and wants to give it to her. It will be a bad lookout for us. How are we going to live, if he gives her the money? They'll turn me out of the house! You try and manage somehow! You said he went to the shed last night.

NIKÍTA  I saw him coming from there, but where he's shoved it to, who can tell?

ANÍSYA  Oh, my poor head! I'll go and have a look there. (NIKÍTA *steps aside.*)

MATRYÓNA  (*Comes out of the hut and down the steps of the porch to* ANÍSYA *and* NIKÍTA.) Don't go anywhere. He's got the money on him. I felt it on a string round his neck.

ANÍSYA  Oh my head, my head!

MATRYÓNA  If you don't keep wide awake now, then you may whistle for it. If his sister comes—then goodbye to it!

ANÍSYA  That's true. She'll come and he'll give it her. What's to be done? Oh my poor head!

MATRYÓNA  What is to be done? Why, look here; the samovar is boiling, go and make the tea and pour him out a cup, and then (*whispers*) put in all that's left in the paper. When he's drunk the cup, then just take it. He'll not tell, no fear.

ANÍSYA  Oh! I'm afeared!

MATRYÓNA  Don't be talking now, but look alive, and I'll keep his sister off if need be. Mind, don't make a blunder! Get hold of the money and bring it here, and Nikíta will hide it.

ANÍSYA  Oh my head, my head! I don't know how I'm going to...

MATRYÓNA  Don't talk about it I tell you, do as I bid you. Nikíta!

NIKÍTA  What is it?

MATRYÓNA  You stay here—sit down—in case something is wanted.

NIKÍTA  (*Waves his hand.*) Oh these women, what won't they be up to? Muddle one up completely. Bother them! I'll really go and fetch out the potatoes.

MATRYÓNA  (*Catches him by the arm.*) Stay here, I tell you.

(NAN *enters.*)

ANÍSYA  Well?

NAN  She was down in her daughter's vegetable plot—she's coming.

ANÍSYA  Coming! What shall we do?

MATRYÓNA  There's plenty of time if you do as I tell you.

ANÍSYA   I don't know what to do; I know nothing, my brain's all in a whirl. Nan! Go, daughter, and see to the calves, they'll have run away, I'm afraid.... Oh dear, I haven't the courage.

MATRYÓNA   Go on! I should think the samovar's boiling over.

ANÍSYA   Oh my head, my poor head! (*Exit.*)

MATRYÓNA   (*Approaches* NIKÍTA.) Now then, sonnie. (*Sits down beside him.*) Your affairs must also be thought about, and not left anyhow.

NIKÍTA   What affairs?

MATRYÓNA   Why, this affair—how you're to live your life.

NIKÍTA   How to live my life? Others live, and I shall live!

MATRYÓNA   The old man will probably die today.

NIKÍTA   Well, if he dies, God give him rest! What's that to me?

MATRYÓNA   (*Keeps looking towards the porch while she speaks.*) Eh, sonnie! Those that are alive have to think about living. One needs plenty of sense in these matters, honey. What do you think? I've tramped all over the place after your affairs, I've got quite footsore bothering about matters. And you must not forget me when the time comes.

NIKÍTA   And what's it you've been bothering about?

MATRYÓNA   About your affairs, about your future. If you don't take trouble in good time you'll get nothing. You know Iván Moséitch? Well, I've been to him too. I went there the other day. I had something else to settle, you know. Well, so I sat and chatted awhile and then came to the point. "Tell me, Iván Moséitch," says I, "how's one to manage an affair of this kind? Supposing," says I, "a peasant as is a widower married a second wife, and supposing all the children he has is a daughter by the first wife, and a daughter by the second. Then," says I, "when that peasant dies, could an outsider get hold of the homestead by marrying the widow? Could he," says I, "give both the daughters in marriage and remain master of the house himself?" "Yes, he could," says he, "but," says he, "it would mean a deal of trouble; still the thing could be managed by means of money, but if there's no money it's no good trying."

NIKÍTA (*Laughs.*) That goes without saying, only fork out the money. Who does not want money?

MATRYÓNA Well then, honey, so I spoke out plainly about the affair. And he says, "First and foremost, your son will have to get himself on the register of that village—that will cost something. The elders will have to be treated. And they, you see, they'll sign. Everything," says he, "must be done sensibly." Look, (*unwraps her kerchief and takes out a paper*) he's written out this paper; just read it, you're a scholar, you know. (NIKÍTA *reads.*)

NIKÍTA   This paper's only a decision for the elders to sign. There's no great wisdom needed for that.

MATRYÓNA   But you just hear what Iván Moséitch bids us do. "Above all," he says, "mind and don't let the money slip away, dame. If she don't get hold of the money," he says, "they'll not let her do it. Money's the great thing!" So look out, sonnie, things are coming to a head.

NIKÍTA   What's that to me? The money's hers—so let her look out.

MATRYÓNA   Ah, sonnie, how you look at it! How can a woman manage such affairs? Even if she does get the money, is she capable of arranging it all? One knows what a woman is! You're a man anyhow. You can hide it, and all that. You see, you've after all got more sense, in case of anything happening.

NIKÍTA   Oh, your woman's notions are all so inexpedient!

MATRYÓNA   Why inexpedient? You just collar the money, and the woman's in your hands. And then should she ever turn snappish you'd be able to tighten the reins!

NIKÍTA   Bother you all—I'm going.

ANÍSYA   (*Quite pale, runs out of the hut and round the corner to* MATRYÓNA.) So it was, it was on him! Here it is! (*Shows that she has something under her apron.*)

MATRYÓNA   Give it to Nikíta, he'll hide it. Nikíta, take it

|  |  |
|---|---|
| | and hide it somewhere. |
| NIKÍTA | All right, give here! |
| ANÍSYA | O-oh, my poor head! No, I'd better do it myself. (*Goes towards the gate.*) |
| MATRYÓNA | (*Seizing her by the arm.*) Where are you going to? You'll be missed. There's the sister coming; give it him; he knows what to do. Eh, you blockhead! |
| ANÍSYA | (*Stops irresolutely.*) Oh, my head, my head! |
| NIKÍTA | Well, give it here. I'll shove it away somewhere. |
| ANÍSYA | Where will you shove it to? |
| NIKÍTA | (*Laughing.*) Why, are you afraid? |

(*Enter* AKOULÍNA, *carrying clothes from the wash.*)

|  |  |
|---|---|
| ANÍSYA | O-oh, my poor head! (*Gives the money.*) Mind, Nikíta. |
| NIKÍTA | What are you afraid of? I'll hide it so that I'll not be able to find it myself. (*Exit.*) |
| ANÍSYA | (*Stands in terror.*) Oh dear, and supposing he... |
| MATRYÓNA | Well, is he dead? |
| ANÍSYA | Yes, he seems dead. He did not move when I took it. |
| MATRYÓNA | Go in, there's Akoulína. |
| ANÍSYA | Well there, I've done the sin and he has the money.... |
| MATRYÓNA | Have done and go in! There's Martha coming! |
| ANÍSYA | There now, I've trusted him. What's going to |

|   |   |
|---|---|
| | happen now? (*Exit.*) |
| MARTHA | (*Enters from one side,* AKOULÍNA *enters from the other. To* AKOULÍNA.) I should have come before, but I was at my daughter's. Well, how's the old man? Is he dying? |
| AKOULÍNA | (*Puts down the clothes.*) Don't know, I've been to the river. |
| MARTHA | (*Pointing to* MATRYÓNA.) Who's that? |
| MATRYÓNA | I'm from Zoúevo. I'm Nikíta's mother from Zoúevo, my dearie. Good afternoon to you. He's withering, withering away, poor dear—your brother, I mean. He came out himself. "Send for my sister," he said, "because," said he... Dear me, why, I do believe, he's dead! |
| ANÍSYA | (*Runs out screaming. Clings to a post, and begins wailing.*)[4] Oh, oh, ah! who-o-o-m have you left me to, why-y-y have you dese-e-e-rted me—a miserable widow... to live my life alone... Why have you closed your bright eyes... |
| | (*Enter* NEIGHBOUR. MATRYÓNA *and* NEIGHBOUR *catch hold of* ANÍSYA *under the arms to support her.* AKOULÍNA *and* MARTHA *go into the hut. A crowd assembles.*) |
| A VOICE IN THE CROWD | Send for the old women to lay out the body. |
| MATRYÓNA | (*Rolls up her sleeves.*) Is there any water in the copper? But I daresay the samovar is still hot. I'll also go and help a bit. |

(*Curtain.*)

# Act III

*The same hut. Winter. Nine months have passed since Act II.* ANÍSYA, *plainly dressed, sits before a loom weaving.* NAN *is on the oven.*

MÍTRITCH (*An old labourer, enters, and slowly takes off his outdoor things.*) Oh Lord, have mercy! Well, hasn't the master come home yet?

ANÍSYA What?

MÍTRITCH Nikíta isn't back from town, is he?

ANÍSYA No.

MÍTRITCH Must have been on the spree. Oh Lord!

ANÍSYA Have you finished in the stackyard?

MÍTRITCH What d'you think? Got it all as it should be, and covered everything with straw! I don't like doing things by halves! Oh Lord! holy Nicholas! (*Picks at the corns on his hands.*) But it's time he was back.

ANÍSYA What need has he to hurry? He's got money. Merrymaking with that girl, I daresay...

MÍTRITCH Why shouldn't one make merry if one has the money? And why did Akoulína go to town?

ANÍSYA You'd better ask her. How do I know what the devil took her there!

MÍTRITCH What! to town? There's all sorts of things to be got in town if one's got the means. Oh Lord!

NAN Mother, I heard myself. "I'll get you a little

shawl," he says, blest if he didn't; "you shall choose it yourself," he says. And she got herself up so fine; she put on her velveteen coat and the French shawl.

ANÍSYA  Really, a girl's modesty reaches only to the door. Step over the threshold and it's forgotten. She is a shameless creature.

MÍTRITCH  Oh my! What's the use of being ashamed? While there's plenty of money make merry. Oh Lord! It is too soon to have supper, eh? (ANÍSYA *does not answer.*) I'll go and get warm meanwhile. (*Climbs on the stove.*) Oh Lord! Blessed Virgin Mother! holy Nicholas!

NEIGHBOUR  (*Enters.*) Seems your goodman's not back yet?

ANÍSYA  No.

NEIGHBOUR  It's time he was. Hasn't he perhaps stopped at our inn? My sister, Thekla, says there's heaps of sledges standing there as have come from the town.

ANÍSYA  Nan! Nan, I say!

NAN  Yes?

ANÍSYA  You run to the inn and see! Mayhap, being drunk, he's gone there.

NAN  (*Jumps down from the oven and dresses.*) All right.

NEIGHBOUR  And he's taken Akoulína with him?

ANÍSYA  Else he'd not have had any need of going. It's because of her he's unearthed all the business there. "Must go to the bank," he says; "it's time

|  |  |
|---:|:---|
|  | to receive the payments," he says. But it's all her fooling. |
| NEIGHBOUR | (*Shakes her head.*) It's a bad lookout. (*Silence.*) |
| NAN | (*At the door.*) And if he's there, what am I to say? |
| ANÍSYA | You only see if he's there. |
| NAN | All right. I'll be back in a winking. (*Long silence.*) |
| MÍTRITCH | (*Roars.*) Oh Lord! merciful Nicholas! |
| NEIGHBOUR | (*Starting.*) Oh, how he scared me? Who is it? |
| ANÍSYA | Why, Mítritch, our labourer. |
| NEIGHBOUR | Oh dear, oh dear, what a fright he did give me! I had quite forgotten. But tell me, dear, I've heard someone's been wooing Akoulína? |
| ANÍSYA | (*Gets up from the loom and sits down by the table.*) There was someone from Dédlovo; but it seems the affair's got wind there too. They made a start, and then stopped; so the thing fell through. Of course, who'd care to? |
| NEIGHBOUR | And the Lizounófs from Zoúevo? |
| ANÍSYA | They made some steps too, but it didn't come off either. They won't even see us. |
| NEIGHBOUR | Yet it's time she was married. |
| ANÍSYA | Time and more than time! Ah, my dear, I'm that impatient to get her out of the house; but the matter does not come off. He does not wish it, nor she either. He's not yet had enough of his beauty, you see. |

NEIGHBOUR  Eh, eh, eh, what doings! Only think of it. Why, he's her stepfather!

ANÍSYA  Ah, friend, they've taken me in completely. They've done me so fine it's beyond saying. I, fool that I was, noticed nothing, suspected nothing, and so I married him. I guessed nothing, but they already understood one another.

NEIGHBOUR  Oh dear, what goings on!

ANÍSYA  So it went on from bad to worse, and I see they begin hiding from me. Ah, friend, I was that sick—that sick of my life! It's not as if I didn't love him.

NEIGHBOUR  That goes without saying.

ANÍSYA  Ah, how hard it is to bear such treatment from him! Oh, how it hurts!

NEIGHBOUR  Yes, and I've heard say he's becoming too free with his fists?

ANÍSYA  And that too! There was a time when he was gentle when he'd had a drop. He used to hit out before, but of me he was always fond! But now when he's in a temper he goes for me and is ready to trample me under his feet. The other day he got both hands entangled in my hair so that I could hardly get away. And the girl's worse than a serpent; it's a wonder the earth bears such furies.

NEIGHBOUR  Ah, ah, my dear, now I look at you, you are a sufferer! To suffer like that is no joke. To have

|           | given shelter to a beggar, and he to lead you such a dance! Why don't you pull in the reins? |
|-----------|---|
| ANÍSYA    | Ah, but my dear, if it weren't for my heart! Him as is gone was stern enough, still I could twist him about any way I liked; but with this one I can do nothing. As soon as I see him all my anger goes. I haven't a grain of courage before him; I go about like a drowned hen. |
| NEIGHBOUR | Ah, neighbour, you must be under a spell. I've heard that Matryóna goes in for that sort of thing. It must be her. |
| ANÍSYA    | Yes, dear; I think so myself sometimes. Gracious me, how hurt I feel at times! I'd like to tear him to pieces. But when I set eyes on him, my heart won't go against him. |
| NEIGHBOUR | It's plain you're bewitched. It don't take long to blight a body. There now, when I look at you, what you have dwindled to! |
| ANÍSYA    | Growing a regular spindle-shanks. And just look at that fool Akoulína. Wasn't the girl a regular untidy slattern, and just look at her now! Where has it all come from? Yes, he has fitted her out. She's grown so smart, so puffed up, just like a bubble that's ready to burst. And, though she's a fool, she's got it into her head, "I'm the mistress," she says; "the house is mine; it's me father wanted him to marry." And she's that vicious! Lord help us, when she gets into a rage she's ready to tear the thatch off the house. |

NEIGHBOUR  Oh dear, what a life yours is, now I come to look at you. And yet there's people envying you: "They're rich," they say; but it seems that gold don't keep tears from falling.

ANÍSYA  Much reason for envy indeed! And the riches, too, will soon be made ducks and drakes of. Dear me, how he squanders money!

NEIGHBOUR  But how's it, dear, you've been so simple to give up the money? It's yours.

ANÍSYA  Ah, if you knew all! The thing is that I've made one little mistake.

NEIGHBOUR  Well, if I were you, I'd go straight and have the law of him. The money's yours; how dare he squander it? There's no such rights.

ANÍSYA  They don't pay heed to that nowadays.

NEIGHBOUR  Ah, my dear, now I come to look at you, you've got that weak.

ANÍSYA  Yes, quite weak, dear, quite weak. He's got me into a regular fix. I don't myself know anything. Oh, my poor head!

NEIGHBOUR  (*Listening.*) There's someone coming, I think. (*The door opens and* AKÍM *enters.*)

AKÍM  (*Crosses himself, knocks the snow off his feet, and takes off his coat.*) Peace be to this house! How do you do? Are you well, daughter?

ANÍSYA  How d'you do, father? Do you come straight from home?

AKÍM  I've been a-thinking, I'll go and see what's name, go to see my son, I mean—my son. I didn't start early—had my dinner, I mean; I went, and it's so what d'you call it—so snowy, hard walking, and so there I'm what d'you call it—late, I mean. And my son—is he at home? At home? My son, I mean.

ANÍSYA  No; he's gone to the town.

AKÍM  (*Sits down on a bench.*) I've some business with him, d'you see, some business, I mean. I told him t'other day, told him I was in need—told him, I mean, that our horse was done for, our horse, you see. So we must what d'ye call it, get a horse, I mean, some kind of a horse, I mean. So there, I've come, you see.

ANÍSYA  Nikíta told me. When he comes back you'll have a talk. (*Goes to the oven.*) Have some supper now, and he'll soon come. Mítritch, eh Mítritch, come have your supper.

MÍTRITCH  Oh Lord! merciful Nicholas!

ANÍSYA  Come to supper.

NEIGHBOUR  I shall go now. Good night. (*Exit.*)

MÍTRITCH  (*Gets down from the oven.*) I never noticed how I fell asleep. Oh Lord! gracious Nicholas! How d'you do, Daddy Akím?

AKÍM  Ah, Mítritch! What are you, what d'ye call it, I mean?...

MÍTRITCH  Why, I'm working for your son, Nikíta.

AKÍM  Dear me! What d'ye call... working for my son, I mean. Dear me!

MÍTRITCH  I was living with a tradesman in town, but

drank all I had there. Now I've come back to the village. I've no home, so I've gone into service. (*Gapes.*) Oh Lord!

AKÍM   But how's that, what d'you call it, or what's name, Nikíta, what does he do? Has he some business, I mean besides, that he should hire a labourer, a labourer I mean, hire a labourer?

ANÍSYA   What business should he have? He used to manage, but now he's other things on his mind, so he's hired a labourer.

MÍTRITCH   Why shouldn't he, seeing he has money?

AKÍM   Now that's what d'you call it, that's wrong, I mean, quite wrong, I mean. That's spoiling oneself.

ANÍSYA   Oh, he has got spoilt, that spoilt, it's just awful.

AKÍM   There now, what d'you call it, one thinks how to make things better, and it gets worse I mean. Riches spoil a man, spoil, I mean.

MÍTRITCH   Fatness makes even a dog go mad; how's one not to get spoilt by fat living? Myself now; how I went on with fat living. I drank for three weeks without being sober. I drank my last breeches. When I had nothing left, I gave it up. Now I've determined not to. Bother it!

AKÍM   And where's what d'you call, your old woman?

MÍTRITCH   My old woman has found her right place, old fellow. She's hanging about the gin-shops in

|   |   |
|---|---|
| | town. She's a swell too; one eye knocked out, and the other black, and her muzzle twisted to one side. And she's never sober; drat her! |
| AKÍM | Oh, oh, oh, how's that? |
| MÍTRITCH | And where's a soldier's wife to go? She has found her right place. (*Silence.*) |
| AKÍM | (*To* ANÍSYA.) And Nikíta—has he what d'you call it, taken anything up to town? I mean, anything to sell? |
| ANÍSYA | (*Laying the table and serving up.*) No, he's taken nothing. He's gone to get money from the bank. |
| AKÍM | (*Sitting down to supper.*) Why? D'you wish to put it to another use, the money I mean? |
| ANÍSYA | No, we don't touch it. Only some twenty or thirty roubles as have come due; they must be taken. |
| AKÍM | Must be taken. Why take it, the money I mean? You'll take some today I mean, and some tomorrow; and so you'll what d'you call it, take it all, I mean. |
| ANÍSYA | We get this besides. The money is all safe. |
| AKÍM | All safe? How's that, safe? You take it, and it what d'you call it, it's all safe. How's that? You put a heap of meal into a bin, or a barn, I mean, and go on taking meal, will it remain there what d'you call it, all safe I mean? That's, what d'you call it, it's cheating. You'd better find out, or else they'll cheat you. Safe indeed! |

I mean you what d'ye call... you take it and it remains all safe there?

ANÍSYA  I know nothing about it. Iván Moséitch advised us at the time. "Put the money in the bank," he said, "the money will be safe, and you'll get interest," he said.

MÍTRITCH  (*Having finished his supper.*) That's so. I've lived with a tradesman. They all do like that. Put the money in the bank, then lie down on the oven and it will keep coming in.

AKÍM  That's queer talk. How's that—what d'ye call, coming in, how's that coming in, and they, who do they get it from I mean, the money I mean?

ANÍSYA  They take the money out of the bank.

MÍTRITCH  Get along! 'Tain't a thing a woman can understand! You look here, I'll make it all clear to you. Mind and remember. You see, suppose you've got some money, and I, for instance, have spring coming on, my land's idle, I've got no seeds, or I have to pay taxes. So, you see, I go to you. "Akím," I say, "give us a ten-rouble note, and when I've harvested in autumn I'll return it, and till two acres for you besides, for having obliged me!" And you, seeing I've something to fall back on—a horse say, or a cow—you say, "No, give two or three roubles for the obligation," and there's an end of it. I'm stuck in the mud, and can't do without. So I say, "All right!" and take a tenner. In the autumn, when I've made my turnover, I bring it back, and you squeeze the extra three roubles out of me.

AKÍM  Yes, but that's what peasants do when they what d'ye call it, when they forget God. It's not honest, I mean, it's no good, I mean.

MÍTRITCH  You wait. You'll see it comes just to the same thing. Now don't forget how you've skinned me. And Anísya, say, has got some money lying idle. She does not know what to do with it, besides, she's a woman, and does not know how to use it. She comes to you. "Couldn't you make some profit with my money too?" she says. "Why not?" say you, and you wait. Before the summer I come again and say, "Give me another tenner, and I'll be obliged." Then you find out if my hide isn't all gone, and if I can be skinned again you give me Anísya's money. But supposing I'm clean shorn—have nothing to eat—then you see I can't be fleeced any more, and you say, "Go your way, friend," and you look out for another, and lend him your own and Anísya's money and skin him. That's what the bank is. So it goes round and round. It's a cute thing, old fellow!

AKÍM  (*Excitedly.*) Gracious me, whatever is that like? It's what d'ye call it, it's filthy! The peasants—what d'ye call it, the peasants do so I mean, and know it's, what d'ye call it, a sin! It's what d'you call, not right, not right, I mean. It's filthy! How can people as have learnt... what d'ye call it...

MÍTRITCH  That, old fellow, is just what they're fond of! And remember, them that are stupid, or the women folk, as can't put their money into use themselves, they take it to the bank, and they there, deuce take 'em, clutch hold of it, and with this money they fleece the people. It's a cute thing!

AKÍM  (*Sighing.*) Oh dear, I see, what d'ye call it, without money it's bad, and with money it's worse! How's that? God told us to work, but you, what d'ye call... I mean you put money into the bank and go to sleep, and the money will what d'ye call it, will feed you while you sleep. It's filthy, that's what I call it; it's not right.

MÍTRITCH  Not right? Eh, old fellow, who cares about that nowadays? And how clean they pluck you, too! That's the fact of the matter.

AKÍM  (*Sighs.*) Ah yes, seems the time's what d'ye call it, the time's growing ripe. There, I've had a look at the closets in town. What they've come to! It's all polished and polished I mean, it's fine, it's what d'ye call it, it's like inside an inn. And what's it all for? What's the good of it? Oh, they've forgotten God. Forgotten, I mean. We've forgotten, forgotten God, God I mean! Thank you, my dear, I've had enough.

I'm quite satisfied. (*Rises.* MÍTRITCH *climbs on to the oven.*)

ANÍSYA (*Eats, and collects the dishes.*) If his father would only take him to task! But I'm ashamed to tell him.

AKÍM What d'you say?

ANÍSYA Oh! it's nothing.

(*Enter* NAN.)

AKÍM Here's a good girl, always busy! You're cold, I should think?

NAN Yes, I am, terribly. How d'you do, grandfather?

ANÍSYA Well? Is he there?

NAN No. But Andriyán is there. He's been to town, and he says he saw them at an inn in town. He says Dad's as drunk as drunk can be!

ANÍSYA Do you want anything to eat? Here you are.

NAN (*Goes to the oven.*) Well, it *is* cold. My hands are quite numb. (AKÍM *takes off his leg-bands and bast-shoes.* ANÍSYA *washes up.*)

ANÍSYA Father!

AKÍM Well, what is it?

ANÍSYA And is Marína living well?

AKÍM Yes, she's living all right. The little woman is what d'ye call it, clever and steady; she's living, and what d'ye call it, doing her best. She's all right; the little woman's of the right sort I mean; painstaking and what d'ye call it,

|   |   |
|---|---|
| | submissive; the little woman's all right I mean, all right, you know. |
| ANÍSYA | And is there no talk in your village that a relative of Marína's husband thinks of marrying our Akoulína? Have you heard nothing of it? |
| AKÍM | Ah; that's Mirónof. Yes, the women did chatter something. But I didn't pay heed, you know. It don't interest me I mean, I don't know anything. Yes, the old women did say something, but I've a bad memory, bad memory, I mean. But the Mirónofs are what d'ye call it, they're all right, I mean they're all right. |
| ANÍSYA | I'm that impatient to get her settled. |
| AKÍM | And why? |
| NAN | (*Listens.*) They've come! |
| ANÍSYA | Well, don't you go bothering them. (*Goes on washing the spoons without turning her head.*) |
| NIKÍTA | (*Enters.*) Anísya! Wife! who has come? (ANÍSYA *looks up and turns away in silence.*) |
| NIKÍTA | (*Severely.*) Who has come? Have you forgotten? |
| ANÍSYA | Now don't humbug. Come in! |
| NIKÍTA | (*Still more severely.*) Who's come? |
| ANÍSYA | (*Goes up and takes him by the arm.*) Well then, husband has come. Now then, come in! |
| NIKÍTA | (*Holds back.*) Ah, that's it! Husband! And what's husband called? Speak properly. |

ANÍSYA  Oh bother you! Nikíta!

NIKÍTA  Where have you learnt manners? The full name.

ANÍSYA  Nikíta Akímitch! Now then!

NIKÍTA  (*Still in the doorway.*) Ah, that's it! But now—the surname?

ANÍSYA  (*Laughs and pulls him by the arm.*) Tchilíkin. Dear me, what airs!

NIKÍTA  Ah, that's it. (*Holds on to the doorpost.*) No, now say with which foot Tchilíkin steps into this house!

ANÍSYA  That's enough! You're letting the cold in!

NIKÍTA  Say with which foot he steps? You've got to say it—that's flat.

ANÍSYA  (*Aside.*) He'll go on worrying. (*To* NIKÍTA.) Well then, with the left. Come in!

NIKÍTA  Ah, that's it.

ANÍSYA  You look who's in the hut!

NIKÍTA  Ah, my parent! Well, what of that? I'm not ashamed of my parent. I can pay my respects to my parent. How d'you do, father? (*Bows and puts out his hand.*) My respects to you.

ANÍSYA  Come in!

NIKÍTA  Ah, that's it.

ANÍSYA  You look who's in the hut!

NIKÍTA  Ah, my parent! Well, what of that? I'm not ashamed of my parent.

AKÍM  (*Does not answer.*) Drink, I mean drink, what it

does! It's filthy!

NIKÍTA   Drink, what's that? I've been drinking? I'm to blame, that's flat! I've had a glass with a friend, drank his health.

ANÍSYA   Go and lie down, I say.

NIKÍTA   Wife, say where am I standing?

ANÍSYA   Now then, it's all right, lie down!

NIKÍTA   No, I'll first drink a samovar with my parent. Go and light the samovar. Akoulína, I say, come here!

(*Enter* AKOULÍNA, *smartly dressed and carrying their purchases.*)

AKOULÍNA   Why have you thrown everything about? Where's the yarn?

NIKÍTA   The yarn? The yarn's there. Hullo, Mítritch, where are you? Asleep? Asleep? Go and put the horse up.

AKÍM   (*Not seeing* AKOULÍNA *but looking at his son.*) Dear me, what is he doing? The old man's what d'ye call it, quite done up, I mean—been thrashing—and look at him, what d'ye call it, putting on airs! Put up the horse! Faugh, what filth!

MÍTRITCH   (*Climbs down from the oven, and puts on felt boots.*) Oh, merciful Lord! Is the horse in the yard? Done it to death, I dare say. Just see how he's been swilling, the deuce take him. Up to his very throat. Oh Lord, holy Nicholas! (*Puts on sheepskin, and exit.*)

NIKÍTA (*Sits down.*) You must forgive me, father. It's true I've had a drop; well, what of that? Even a hen will drink. Ain't it true? So you must forgive me. Never mind Mítritch, he doesn't mind, he'll put it up.

ANÍSYA Shall I really light the samovar?

NIKÍTA Light it! My parent has come. I wish to talk to him, and shall drink tea with him. (*To* AKOULÍNA.) Have you brought all the parcels?

AKOULÍNA The parcels? I've brought mine, the rest's in the sledge. Hi, take this, this isn't mine!

(*Throws a parcel on the table and puts the others into her box.* NAN *watches her while she puts them away.* AKÍM *does not look at his son, but puts his leg-bands and bast-shoes on the oven.*)

ANÍSYA (*Going out with the samovar.*) Her box is full as it is, and still he's bought more!

NIKÍTA Have you brought all the parcels?

AKOULÍNA The parcels? I've brought mine, the rest's in the sledge.

ANÍSYA Her box is full as it is, and still he's bought more!

NIKÍTA (*Pretending to be sober.*) You must not be cross with me, father. You think I'm drunk? I am all there, that's flat! As they say, "Drink, but keep your wits about you." I can talk with you at once, father. I can attend to any business. You told me about the money; your horse is worn-out—I remember! That can all be managed.

That's all in our hands. If it was an enormous sum that's wanted, then we might wait; but as it is I can do everything. That's the case.

AKÍM (*Goes on fidgeting with the leg-bands.*) Eh, lad, "It's ill sledging when the thaw has set in."

NIKÍTA What d'you mean by that? "And it's ill talking with one who is drunk"? But don't you worry, let's have some tea. And I can do anything; that's flat! I can put everything to rights.

AKÍM (*Shakes his head.*) Eh, eh, eh!

NIKÍTA The money, here it is. (*Puts his hand in his pocket, pulls out pocketbook, handles the notes in it and takes out a ten-rouble note.*) Take this to get a horse; I can't forget my parent. I shan't forsake him, that's flat. Because he's my parent! Here you are, take it! Really now, I don't grudge it. (*Comes up and pushes the note towards* AKÍM *who won't take it.* NIKÍTA *catches hold of his father's hand.*) Take it, I tell you. I don't grudge it.

AKÍM I can't, what d'you call it, I mean, can't take it! And can't what d'ye call it, talk to you, because you're not yourself, I mean.

NIKÍTA I'll not let you go! Take it! (*Puts the money into* AKÍM's *hand.*)

ANÍSYA (*Enters, and stops.*) You'd better take it, he'll give you no peace!

AKÍM (*Takes it, and shakes his head.*) Oh! that liquor. Not like a man, I mean!

| | |
|---|---|
| NIKÍTA | That's better! If you repay it you'll repay it, if not I'll make no bother. That's what I am! (*Sees* AKOULÍNA.) Akoulína, show your presents. |
| AKOULÍNA | What? |
| NIKÍTA | Show your presents. |
| AKOULÍNA | The presents, what's the use of showing 'em? I've put 'em away. |
| NIKÍTA | Get them, I tell you. Nan will like to see 'em. Undo the shawl. Give it here. |
| AKÍM | Oh, oh! It's sickening! (*Climbs on the oven.*) |
| AKOULÍNA | (*Gets out the parcels and puts them on the table.*) Well, there you are—what's the good of looking at 'em? |
| NAN | Oh how lovely! It's as good as Stepanída's. |
| AKOULÍNA | Stepanída's? What's Stepanída's compared to this? (*Brightening up and undoing the parcels.*) Just look here—see the quality! It's a French one. |
| NAN | The print *is* fine! Mary has a dress like it, only lighter on a blue ground. This *is* pretty. |
| NIKÍTA | Ah, that's it! |
| | (ANÍSYA *passes angrily into the closet, returns with a tablecloth and the chimney of the samovar, and goes up to the table.*) |
| ANÍSYA | Drat you, littering the table! |
| NIKÍTA | You look here! |
| ANÍSYA | What am I to look at? Have I never seen anything? Put it away! (*Sweeps the shawl on to* |

*the floor with her arm.*)

**AKOULÍNA**  What are you pitching things down for? You pitch your own things about! (*Picks up the shawl.*)

**NIKÍTA**  Anísya! Look here!

**ANÍSYA**  Why am I to look?

**NIKÍTA**  You think I have forgotten you? Look here! (*Shows her a parcel and sits down on it.*) It's a present for you. Only you must earn it! Wife, where am I sitting?

**ANÍSYA**  Enough of your humbug. I'm not afraid of you. Whose money are you spreeing on and buying your fat wench presents with? Mine!

**AKOULÍNA**  Yours indeed? No fear! You wished to steal it, but it did not come off! Get out of the way! (*Pushes her while trying to pass.*)

**ANÍSYA**  What are you shoving for? I'll teach you to shove!

**AKOULÍNA**  Shove me? You try! (*Presses against* ANÍSYA.)

**NIKÍTA**  Now then, now then, you women. Have done now! (*Steps between them.*)

**AKOULÍNA**  Comes shoving herself in! You ought to keep quiet and remember your doings! You think no one knows!

**ANÍSYA**  Knows what? Out with it, out with it! What do they know?

**AKOULÍNA**  I know something about you!

**ANÍSYA**  You're a slut who goes with another's

|         |                                                                                  |
|---------|----------------------------------------------------------------------------------|
|         | husband!                                                                         |
| AKOULÍNA | And you did yours to death!                                                     |
| ANÍSYA  | (*Throwing herself on* AKOULÍNA.) You're raving!                                 |
| NIKÍTA  | (*Holding her back.*) Anísya, you seem to have forgotten!                        |
| ANÍSYA  | Want to frighten me! I'm not afraid of you!                                      |
| NIKÍTA  | (*Turns* ANÍSYA *round and pushes her out.*) Be off!                             |
| ANÍSYA  | Where am I to go? I'll not go out of my own house!                               |
| NIKÍTA  | Be off, I tell you, and don't dare to come in here!                              |
| ANÍSYA  | I won't go! (NIKÍTA *pushes her,* ANÍSYA *cries and screams and clings to the door.*) What! am I to be turned out of my own house by the scruff of the neck? What are you doing, you scoundrel? Do you think there's no law for you? You wait a bit! |
| NIKÍTA  | Now then!                                                                        |
| ANÍSYA  | I'll go to the Elder! To the policeman!                                          |
| NIKÍTA  | Off, I tell you! (*Pushes her out.*)                                             |
| ANÍSYA  | (*Behind the door.*) I'll hang myself!                                           |
| NIKÍTA  | No fear!                                                                         |
| NAN     | Oh, oh, oh! Mother, dear, darling! (*Cries.*)                                    |
| NIKÍTA  | Me frightened of her! A likely thing! What are you crying for? She'll come back, no fear. Go and see to the samovar. (*Exit* NAN.) |
| AKOULÍNA | (*Collects and folds her presents.*) The mean                                   |

wretch, how she's messed it up. But wait a bit, I'll cut up her jacket for her! Sure I will!

NIKÍTA   I've turned her out, what more do you want?

AKOULÍNA   She's dirtied my new shawl. If that bitch hadn't gone away, I'd have torn her eyes out!

NIKÍTA   That's enough. Why should you be angry? Now if I loved her...

AKOULÍNA   Loved her? She's worth loving, with her fat mug! If you'd have given her up, then nothing would have happened. You should have sent her to the devil. And the house was mine all the same, and the money was mine! Says she is the mistress, but what sort of mistress is she to her husband? She's a murderess, that's what she is! She'll serve you the same way!

NIKÍTA   Oh dear, how's one to stop a woman's jaw? You don't yourself know what you're jabbering about!

AKOULÍNA   Yes, I do. I'll not live with her! I'll turn her out of the house! She can't live here with me. The mistress indeed! She's not the mistress—that jailbird!

NIKÍTA   That's enough! What have you to do with her? Don't mind her. You look at me! I am the master! I do as I like. I've ceased to love her, and now I love you. I love who I like! The power is mine, she's under me. That's where I keep her. (*Points to his feet.*) A pity we've no concertina. (*Sings.*)

"We have loaves on the stoves,
We have porridge on the shelf.
So we'll live and be gay,
Making merry every day,
And when death comes,
Then we'll die!
We have loaves on the stoves,
We have porridge on the shelf..."

(*Enter* MÍTRITCH. *He takes off his outdoor things and climbs on the oven.*)

MÍTRITCH  Seems the women have been fighting again! Tearing each other's hair. Oh Lord, gracious Nicholas!

AKÍM  (*Sitting on the edge of the oven, takes his leg-bands and shoes and begins putting them on.*) Get in, get into the corner.

MÍTRITCH  Seems they can't settle matters between them. Oh Lord!

NIKÍTA  Get out the liquor, we'll have some with our tea.

NAN  (*To* AKOULÍNA.) Sister, the samovar is just boiling over.

NIKÍTA  And where's your mother?

NAN  She's standing and crying out there in the passage.

NIKÍTA  Oh, that's it! Call her, and tell her to bring the samovar. And you, Akoulína, get the tea things.

AKOULÍNA  The tea things? All right. (*Brings the things.*)

NIKÍTA (*Unpacks spirits, rusks, and salt herrings.*) That's for myself. This is yarn for the wife. The paraffin is out there in the passage, and here's the money. Wait a bit, (*takes a counting-frame*) I'll add it up. (*Adds.*) Wheat-flour, eighty kopecks, oil... Father, ten roubles.... Father, come let's have some tea!

(*Silence.* AKÍM *sits on the oven and winds the bands round his legs. Enter* ANÍSYA *with samovar.*)

ANÍSYA Where shall I put it?

NIKÍTA Here on the table. Well! have you been to the Elder? Ah, that's it! Have your say and then eat your words. Now then, that's enough. Don't be cross, sit down and drink this. (*Fills a wineglass for her.*) And here's your present. (*Gives her the parcel he had been sitting on.* ANÍSYA *takes it silently and shakes her head.*)

AKÍM (*Gets down and puts on his sheepskin, then comes up to the table and puts down the money.*) Here, take your money back! Put it away.

NIKÍTA (*Does not see the money.*) Why have you put on your things?

AKÍM I'm going, going I mean; forgive me for the Lord's sake. (*Takes up his cap and belt.*)

NIKÍTA My gracious! Where are you going to at this time of night?

AKÍM I can't, I mean what d'ye call 'em, in your

house, what d'ye call 'em, can't stay I mean, stay, can't stay, forgive me.

NIKÍTA  But are you going without having any tea?

AKÍM  (*Fastens his belt.*) Going, because, I mean, it's not right in your house, I mean, what d'you call it, not right, Nikíta, in the house, what d'ye call it, not right! I mean, you are living a bad life, Nikíta, bad—I'll go.

NIKÍTA  Eh now! Have done talking! Sit down and drink your tea!

ANÍSYA  Why, father, you'll shame us before the neighbours. What has offended you?

AKÍM  Nothing what d'ye call it, nothing has offended me, nothing at all! I mean only, I see, what d'you call it, I mean, I see my son, to ruin I mean, to ruin, I mean my son's on the road to ruin, I mean.

NIKÍTA  What ruin? Just prove it!

AKÍM  Ruin, ruin; you're in the midst of it! What did I tell you that time?

NIKÍTA  You said all sorts of things!

AKÍM  I told you, what d'ye call it, I told you about the orphan lass. That you had wronged an orphan—Marína, I mean, wronged her!

NIKÍTA  Eh! he's at it again. Let bygones be bygones... All that's past!

AKÍM  (*Excited.*) Past! No, lad, it's not past. Sin, I mean, fastens on to sin—drags sin after it, and you've stuck fast, Nikíta, fast in sin! Stuck fast in sin! I see you're fast in sin. Stuck fast, sunk in sin, I mean!

NIKÍTA  Sit down and drink your tea, and have done with it!

AKÍM  I can't, I mean can't what d'ye call it, can't drink tea. Because of your filth, I mean; I feel what d'ye call it, I feel sick, very sick! I can't what d'ye call it, I can't drink tea with you.

NIKÍTA  Eh! There he goes rambling! Come to the table.

AKÍM  You're in your riches same as in a net—you're in a net, I mean. Ah, Nikíta, it's the soul that God needs!

NIKÍTA  Now really, what right have you to reprove me in my own house? Why do you keep on at me? Am I a child that you can pull by the hair? Nowadays those things have been dropped!

AKÍM  That's true. I have heard that nowadays, what d'ye call it, that nowadays children pull their fathers' beards, I mean! But that's ruin, that's ruin, I mean!

NIKÍTA  (*Angrily.*) We are living without help from you, and it's you who came to us with your wants!

AKÍM  The money? There's your money! I'll go begging, begging I mean, before I'll take it, I mean.

NIKÍTA  That's enough! Why be angry and upset the whole company! (*Holds him by the arm.*)

| | |
|---:|:---|
| AKÍM | (*Shrieks.*) Let go! I'll not stay. I'd rather sleep under some fence than in the midst of your filth! Faugh! God forgive me! (*Exit.*) |
| NIKÍTA | Here's a go! |
| AKÍM | (*Reopens the door.*) Come to your senses, Nikíta! It's the soul that God wants! (*Exit.*) |
| AKOULÍNA | (*Takes cups.*) Well, shall I pour out the tea? (*Takes a cup. All are silent.*) |
| MÍTRITCH | (*Roars.*) Oh Lord, be merciful to me a sinner! (*All start.*) |
| NIKÍTA | (*Lies down on the bench.*) Oh, it's dull, it's dull! (*To* AKOULÍNA.) Where's the concertina? |
| AKOULÍNA | The concertina? He's bethought himself of it. Why, you took it to be mended. I've poured out your tea. Drink it! |
| NIKÍTA | I don't want it! Put out the light... Oh, how dull I feel, how dull! (*Sobs.*) |

(*Curtain.*)

# Act IV

Autumn. Evening. The moon is shining. The stage represents the interior of courtyard. The scenery at the back shows, in the middle, the back porch of the hut. To the right the winter half of the hut and the gate; to the left the summer half and the cellar. To the right of the stage is a shed. The sound of tipsy voices and shouts are heard from the hut.[5] SECOND NEIGHBOUR WOMAN *comes out of the hut and beckons to* FIRST NEIGHBOUR WOMAN.

SECOND NEIGHBOUR: How's it Akoulína has not shown herself?

FIRST NEIGHBOUR: Why hasn't she shown herself? She'd have been glad to; but she's too ill, you know. The suitor's relatives have come, and want to see the girl; and she, my dear, she's lying in the cold hut and can't come out, poor thing!

SECOND NEIGHBOUR: But how's that?

FIRST NEIGHBOUR: They say she's been bewitched by an evil eye! She's got pains in the stomach!

SECOND NEIGHBOUR: You don't say so?

FIRST NEIGHBOUR: What else could it be? (*Whispers.*)

SECOND: Dear me! There's a go! But his relatives will

| | |
|---|---|
| NEIGHBOUR | surely find it out? |
| FIRST NEIGHBOUR | They find it out! They're all drunk! Besides, they are chiefly after her dowry. Just think what they give with the girl! Two furs, my dear, six dresses, a French shawl, and I don't know how many pieces of linen, and money as well—two hundred roubles, it's said! |
| SECOND NEIGHBOUR | That's all very well, but even money can't give much pleasure in the face of such a disgrace. |
| FIRST NEIGHBOUR | Hush!... There's his father, I think. |

(*They cease talking, and go into the hut.*)

(*The Suitor's Father comes out of the hut hiccuping.*)

| | |
|---|---|
| THE FATHER | Oh, I'm all in a sweat. It's awfully hot! Will just cool myself a bit. (*Stands puffing.*) The Lord only knows what—something is not right. I can't feel happy.—Well, it's the old woman's affair. |

(*Enter* MATRYÓNA *from hut.*)

| | |
|---|---|
| MATRYÓNA | And I was just thinking, where's the father? Where's the father? And here you are, dear friend.... Well, dear friend, the Lord be thanked! Everything is as honourable as can be! When one's arranging a match one should not boast. And I have never learnt to boast. But as you've come about the right business, so with the Lord's help, you'll be grateful to |

me all your life! She's a wonderful girl! There's no other like her in all the district!

THE FATHER   That's true enough, but how about the money?

MATRYÓNA   Don't you trouble about the money! All she had from her father goes with her. And it's more than one gets easily, as things are nowadays. Three times fifty roubles!

THE FATHER   We don't complain, but it's for our own child. Naturally we want to get the best we can.

MATRYÓNA   I'll tell you straight, friend: if it hadn't been for me, you'd never have found anything like her! They've had an offer from the Karmílins, but I stood out against it. And as for the money, I'll tell you truly: when her father, God be merciful to his soul, was dying, he gave orders that the widow should take Nikíta into the homestead—of course I know all about it from my son—and the money was to go to Akoulína. Why, another one might have thought of his own interests, but Nikíta gives everything clean! It's no trifle. Fancy what a sum it is!

THE FATHER   People are saying, that more money was left her? The lad's sharp too!

MATRYÓNA   Oh, dear soul alive! A slice in another's hand always looks big; all she had will be handed over. I tell you, throw doubts to the wind and make all sure! What a girl she is! as fresh as a daisy!

THE FATHER: That's so. But my old woman and I were only wondering about the girl; why has she not come out? We've been thinking, suppose she's sickly?

MATRYÓNA: Oh, ah.... Who? She? Sickly? Why, there's none to compare with her in the district. The girl's as sound as a bell; you can't pinch her. But you saw her the other day! And as for work, she's wonderful! She's a bit deaf, that's true, but there are spots on the sun, you know. And her not coming out, you see, it's from an evil eye! A spell's been cast on her! And I know the bitch who's done the business! They know of the betrothal and they bewitched her. But I know a counter-spell. The girl will get up tomorrow. Don't you worry about the girl!

THE FATHER: Well, of course, the thing's settled.

MATRYÓNA: Yes, of course! Don't you turn back. And don't forget me, I've had a lot of trouble. Don't forget...

(*A woman's voice from the hut.*)

VOICE: If we are to go, let's go. Come along, Iván!

THE FATHER: I'm coming. (*Exeunt. Guests crowd together in the passage and prepare to go away.*)

NAN: (*Runs out of the hut and calls to* ANÍSYA.) Mother!

ANÍSYA: (*From inside.*) What d'you want?

NAN: Mother, come here, or they'll hear.

(ANÍSYA *enters and they go together to the shed.*)

ANÍSYA   Well? What is it? Where's Akoulína?

NAN   She's gone into the barn. It's awful what's she's doing there! I'm blest! "I can't bear it," she says. "I'll scream," she says, "I'll scream out loud." Blest if she didn't.

ANÍSYA   She'll have to wait. We'll see our visitors off first.

NAN   Oh mother! She's so bad! And she's angry too. "What's the good of their drinking my health?" she says. "I shan't marry," she says. "I shall die," she says. Mother, supposing she does die! It's awful. I'm so frightened!

ANÍSYA   No fear, she'll not die. But don't you go near her. Come along. (*Exit* ANÍSYA *and* NAN.)

MÍTRITCH   (*Comes in at the gate and begins collecting the scattered hay.*) Oh Lord! Merciful Nicholas! What a lot of liquor they've been and swilled, and the smell they've made! It smells even out here! But no, I don't want any, drat it! See how they've scattered the hay about. They don't eat it, but only trample it under foot. A truss gone before you know it. Oh, that smell, it seems to be just under my nose! Drat it! (*Yawns.*) It's time to go to sleep! But I don't care to go into the hut. It seems to float just round my nose! It has a strong scent, the damned stuff! (*The guests are heard driving off.*) They're off at last. Oh Lord! Merciful Nicholas! There they go, binding themselves and gulling one another. And it's all gammon!

(*Enter* NIKÍTA.)

NIKÍTA. Mítritch, you get off to sleep and I'll put this straight.

MÍTRITCH. All right, you throw it to the sheep. Well, have you seen 'em all off?

NIKÍTA. Yes, they're off! But things are not right! I don't know what to do!

MÍTRITCH. It's a fine mess. But there's the Foundlings'[6] for that sort of thing. Whoever likes may drop one there; they'll take 'em all. Give 'em as many as you like, they ask no questions, and even pay—if the mother goes in as a wet-nurse. It's easy enough nowadays.

NIKÍTA. But mind, Mítritch, don't go blabbing.

MÍTRITCH. It's no concern of mine. Cover the tracks as you think best. Dear me, how you smell of liquor! I'll go in. Oh Lord! (*Exit, yawning.*)

(NIKÍTA *is long silent. Sits down on a sledge.*)

NIKÍTA. Here's a go!

(*Enter* ANÍSYA.)

ANÍSYA. Where are you?

NIKÍTA. Here.

ANÍSYA. What are you doing there? There's no time to be lost! We must take it out directly!

NIKÍTA. What are we to do?

ANÍSYA. I'll tell you what you are to do. And you'll

|  |  |
|---|---|
|  | have to do it! |
| NIKÍTA | You'd better take it to the Foundlings'—if anything. |
| ANÍSYA | Then you'd better take it there yourself if you like! You've a hankering for smut, but you're weak when it comes to settling up, I see! |
| NIKÍTA | What's to be done? |
| ANÍSYA | Go down into the cellar, I tell you, and dig a hole! |
| NIKÍTA | Couldn't you manage, somehow, some other way? |
| ANÍSYA | (*Imitating him.*) "Some other way?" Seems we can't "some other way!" You should have thought about it a year ago. Do what you're told to! |
| NIKÍTA | Oh dear, what a go! |

(*Enter* NAN.)

|  |  |
|---|---|
| NAN | Mother! Grandmother's calling! I think sister's got a baby! I'm blest if it didn't scream! |
| ANÍSYA | What are you babbling about? Plague take you! It's kittens whining there. Go into the hut and sleep, or I'll give it you! |
| NAN | Mammy dear, truly, I swear… |
| ANÍSYA | (*Raising her arm as if to strike.*) I'll give it you! You be off and don't let me catch sight of you! (NAN *runs into hut. To* NIKÍTA.) Do as you're told, or else mind! (*Exit.*) |
| NIKÍTA | (*Alone. After a long silence.*) Here's a go! Oh |

these women! What a fix! Says you should have thought of it a year ago. When's one to think beforehand? When's one to think? Why, last year this Anísya dangled after me. What was I to do? Am I a monk? The master died; and I covered my sin as was proper, so I was not to blame there. Aren't there lots of such cases? And then those powders. Did I put her up to that? Why, had I known what the bitch was up to, I'd have killed her! I'm sure I should have killed her! She's made me her partner in these horrors—that jade! And she became loathsome to me from that day! She became loathsome, loathsome to me as soon as mother told me about it. I can't bear the sight of her! Well then, how could I live with her? And then it begun.... That wench began hanging round. Well, what was I to do! If I had not done it, someone else would. And this is what comes of it! Still I'm not to blame in this either. Oh, what a go! (*Sits thinking.*) They are bold, these women! What a plan to think of! But I won't have a hand in it!

(*Enter* MATRYÓNA *with a lantern and spade, panting.*)

MATRYÓNA  Why are you sitting there like a hen on a perch? What did your wife tell you to do? You just get things ready!

NIKÍTA  What do you mean to do?

MATRYÓNA  We know what to do. You do your share!

NIKÍTA   You'll be getting me into a mess!

MATRYÓNA   What? You're not thinking of backing out, are you? Now it's come to this, and you back out!

NIKÍTA   Think what a thing it would be! It's a living soul.

MATRYÓNA   A living soul indeed! Why, it's more dead than alive. And what's one to do with it? Go and take it to the Foundlings'—it will die just the same, and the rumour will get about, and people will talk, and the girl be left on our hands.

NIKÍTA   And supposing it's found out?

MATRYÓNA   Not manage to do it in one's own house? We'll manage it so that no one will have an inkling. Only do as I tell you. We women can't do it without a man. There, take the spade, and get it done there—I'll hold the light.

NIKÍTA   What am I to get done?

MATRYÓNA   (*In a low voice.*) Dig a hole; then we'll bring it out and get it out of the way in a trice! There, she's calling again. Now then, get in, and I'll go.

NIKÍTA   Is it dead then?

MATRYÓNA   Of course it is. Only you must be quick, or else people will notice! They'll see or they'll hear! The rascals must needs know everything. And the policeman went by this evening. Well then, you see (*gives him the spade*), you get down into the cellar and dig a hole right in the corner; the earth is soft there, and you'll smooth it over. Mother earth will not blab to anyone; she'll keep it close. Go then; go, dear.

NIKÍTA  You'll get me into a mess, bother you! I'll go away! You do it alone as best you can!

ANÍSYA  (*Through the doorway.*) Well? Has he dug it?

MATRYÓNA  Why have you come away? What have you done with it?

ANÍSYA  I've covered it with rags. No one can hear it. Well, has he dug it?

MATRYÓNA  He doesn't want to!

ANÍSYA  (*Springs out enraged.*) Doesn't want to! How will he like feeding vermin in prison! I'll go straight away and tell everything to the police! It's all the same if one must perish. I'll go straight and tell!

NIKÍTA  (*Taken aback.*) What will you tell?

ANÍSYA  What? Everything! Who took the money? You! (NIKÍTA *is silent.*) And who gave the poison? I did! But you knew! You knew! You knew! We were in agreement!

MATRYÓNA  That's enough now. Nikíta dear, why are you obstinate? What's to be done now? One must take some trouble. Go, honey.

ANÍSYA  See the fine gentleman! He doesn't like it! You've put upon me long enough! You've trampled me under foot! Now it's my turn! Go, I tell you, or else I'll do what I said.... There, take the spade; there, now go!

NIKÍTA    Drat you! Can't you leave a fellow alone! (*Takes the spade, but shrinks.*) If I don't choose to, I'll not go!

ANÍSYA    Not go? (*Begins to shout.*) Neighbours! Heh! heh!

MATRYÓNA    (*Closes her mouth.*) What are you about? You're mad! He'll go.... Go, sonnie; go, my own.

ANÍSYA    I'll cry murder!

NIKÍTA    Now stop! Oh what people! You'd better be quick.... As well be hung for a sheep as a lamb! (*Goes towards the cellar.*)

MATRYÓNA    Yes, that's just it, honey. If you know how to amuse yourself, you must know how to hide the consequences.

ANÍSYA    (*Still excited.*) He's trampled on me... he and his slut! But it's enough! I'm not going to be the only one! Let him also be a murderer! Then he'll know how it feels!

MATRYÓNA    There, there! How she flares up! Don't you be cross, lass, but do things quietly little by little, as it's best. You go to the girl, and he'll do the work. (*Follows* NIKÍTA *to the cellar with a lantern. He descends into the cellar.*)

ANÍSYA    And I'll make him strangle his dirty brat! (*Still excited.*) I've worried myself to death all alone, with Peter's bones weighing on my mind! Let him feel it too! I'll not spare myself; I've said I'll not spare myself!

NIKÍTA    (*From the cellar.*) Show a light!

MATRYÓNA  (*Holds up the lantern to him. To* ANÍSYA.) He's digging. Go and bring it.

ANÍSYA    You stay with him, or he'll go away, the wretch! And I'll go and bring it.

MATRYÓNA  Mind, don't forget to baptize it, or I will if you like. Have you a cross?

ANÍSYA    I'll find one. I know how to do it. (*Exit.*)

See at end of Act, Variation, which may be used instead of the following.

MATRYÓNA  How the woman bristled up! But one must allow she's been put upon. Well, but with the Lord's help, when we've covered this business, there'll be an end of it. We'll shove the girl off without any trouble. My son will live in comfort. The house, thank God, is as full as an egg. They'll not forget me either. Where would they have been without Matryóna? They'd not have known how to contrive things. (*Peering into the cellar.*) Is it ready, sonnie?

NIKÍTA    (*Puts out his head.*) What are you about there? Bring it quick! What are you dawdling for? If it is to be done, let it be done.

MATRYÓNA  (*Goes towards door of the hut and meets* ANÍSYA. ANÍSYA *comes out with a baby wrapped in rags.*) Well, have you baptized it?

ANÍSYA    Why, of course! It was all I could do to take it away—she wouldn't give it up! (*Comes forward and hands it to* NIKÍTA.)

NIKÍTA  (*Does not take it.*) You bring it yourself!

ANÍSYA  Take it, I tell you! (*Throws the baby to him.*)

NIKÍTA  (*Catches it.*) It's alive! Gracious me, it's moving! It's alive! What am I to...

ANÍSYA  (*Snatches the baby from him and throws it into the cellar.*) Be quick and smother it, and then it won't be alive! (*Pushes* NIKÍTA *down.*) It's your doing, and you must finish it.

MATRYÓNA  (*Sits on the doorstep of the hut.*) He's tenderhearted. It's hard on him, poor dear. Well, what of that? Isn't it also his sin?

(ANÍSYA *stands by the cellar.*)

MATRYÓNA  (*Sits looking at her and discourses.*) Oh, oh, oh! How frightened he was: well, but what of that? If it *is* hard, it's the only thing to be done. Where was one to put it? And just think, how often it happens that people pray to God to have children! But no, God gives them none; or they are all stillborn. Look at our priest's wife now.... And here, where it's not wanted, here it lives. (*Looks towards the cellar.*) I suppose he's finished. (*To* ANÍSYA.) Well?

ANÍSYA  (*Looking into the cellar.*) He's put a board on it and is sitting on it. It must be finished!

MATRYÓNA  Oh, oh! One would be glad not to sin, but what's one to do?

(*Re-enter* NIKÍTA *from cellar, trembling all over.*)

NIKÍTA  It's still alive! I can't! It's alive!

ANÍSYA  If it's alive, where are you off to? (*Tries to stop him.*)

NIKÍTA (*Rushes at her.*) Go away! I'll kill you! (*Catches hold of her arms; she escapes, he runs after her with the spade.* MATRYÓNA *runs towards him and stops him.* ANÍSYA *runs into the porch.* MATRYÓNA *tries to wrench the spade from him. To his mother.*) I'll kill you! I'll kill you! Go away! (MATRYÓNA *runs to* ANÍSYA *in the porch.* NIKÍTA *stops.*) I'll kill you! I'll kill you all!

MATRYÓNA That's because he's so frightened! Never mind, it will pass!

NIKÍTA What have they made me do? What have they made me do? How it whimpered.... How it crunched under me! What have they done with me?... And it's really alive, still alive! (*Listens in silence.*) It's whimpering... There, it's whimpering. (*Runs to the cellar.*)

MATRYÓNA (*To* ANÍSYA.) He's going; it seems he means to bury it. Nikíta, you'd better take the lantern!

NIKÍTA (*Does not heed her, but listens by the cellar door.*) I can hear nothing! I suppose it was fancy! (*Moves away, then stops.*) How the little bones crunched under me. Krr... kr... What have they made me do? (*Listens again.*) Again whimpering! It's really whimpering! What can it be? Mother! Mother, I say! (*Goes up to her.*)

MATRYÓNA What is it, sonnie?

NIKÍTA Mother, my own mother, I can't do any more! Can't do any more! My own mother, have some pity on me!

MATRYÓNA  Oh dear, how frightened you are, my darling! Come, come, drink a drop to give you courage!

NIKÍTA  Mother, mother! It seems my time has come! What have you done with me? How the little bones crunched, and how it whimpered! My own mother! What have you done with me? (*Steps aside and sits down on the sledge.*)

MATRYÓNA  Come, my own, have a drink! It certainly does seem uncanny at nighttime. But wait a bit. When the day breaks, you know, and one day and another passes, you'll forget even to think of it. Wait a bit; when the girl's married we'll even forget to think of it. But you go and have a drink; have a drink! I'll go and put things straight in the cellar myself.

NIKÍTA  (*Rouses himself.*) Is there any drink left? Perhaps I can drink it off! (*Exit.*)

(ANÍSYA, *who has stood all the time by the door, silently makes way for him.*)

MATRYÓNA  Go, go, honey, and I'll set to work! I'll go down myself and dig! Where has he thrown the spade to? (*Finds the spade, and goes down into the cellar.*) Anísya, come here! Hold the light, will you?

ANÍSYA  And what of him?

MATRYÓNA  He's so frightened! You've been too hard with him. Leave him alone, he'll come to his senses. God help him! I'll set to work myself. Put the lantern down here. I can see.

ANÍSYA (*Looking towards the door by which* NIKÍTA *entered the hut.*) Well, have you had enough spree? You've been puffing yourself up, but now you'll know how it feels! You'll lose some of your bluster!

NIKÍTA (*Rushes out of the hut towards the cellar.*) Mother! mother, I say!

MATRYÓNA (*Puts out her head.*) What is it, sonnie?

NIKÍTA (*Listening.*) Don't bury it, it's alive! Don't you hear? Alive! There—it's whimpering! There... quite plain!

MATRYÓNA How can it whimper? Why, you've flattened it into a pancake! The whole head is smashed to bits!

NIKÍTA What is it then? (*Stops his ears.*) It's still whimpering! I am lost! Lost! What have they done with me?... Where shall I go? (*Sits down on the step.*)

(*Curtain.*)

## **Variation**

Instead of the end of Act IV the following variation may be read, and is the one usually acted.

### Scene II

The interior of the hut as in Act I.

NAN lies on the bench, and is covered with a coat. MÍTRITCH is sitting on the oven smoking.

MÍTRITCH  Dear me! How they've made the place smell! Drat 'em! They've been spilling the fine stuff. Even tobacco don't get rid of the smell! It keeps tickling one's nose so. Oh Lord! But it's bedtime, I guess. (*Approaches the lamp to put it out.*)

NAN  (*Jumps up, and remains sitting up.*) Daddy dear,[7] don't put it out!

MÍTRITCH  Not put it out? Why?

NAN  Didn't you hear them making a row in the yard? (*Listens.*) D'you hear, there in the barn again now?

MÍTRITCH  What's that to you? I guess no one's asked you to mind! Lie down and sleep! And I'll turn down the light. (*Turns down lamp.*)

NAN  Daddy darling! Don't put it right out; leave a little bit if only as big as a mouse's eye, else it's so frightening!

MÍTRITCH  (*Laughs.*) All right, all right. (*Sits down by her.*) What's there to be afraid of?

NAN  How can one help being frightened, daddy! Sister did go on so! She was beating her head against the box! (*Whispers.*) You know, I know... a little baby is going to be born.... It's already born, I think....

MÍTRITCH  Eh, what a little busybody it is! May the frogs kick her! Must needs know everything. Lie down and sleep! (NAN *lies down.*) That's right!

(*Tucks her up.*) That's right! There now, if you know too much you'll grow old too soon.

NAN  And you are going to lie on the oven?

MÍTRITCH  Well, of course! What a little silly you are, now I come to look at you! Must needs know everything. (*Tucks her up again, then stands up to go.*) There now, lie still and sleep! (*Goes up to the oven.*)

NAN  It gave just one cry, and now there's nothing to be heard.

MÍTRITCH  Oh Lord! Gracious Nicholas! What is it you can't hear?

NAN  The baby.

MÍTRITCH  There is none, that's why you can't hear it.

NAN  But I heard it! Blest if I didn't hear it! Such a thin voice!

MÍTRITCH  Heard indeed! Much you heard! Well, if you know—why then it was just such a little girl as you that the bogey popped into his bag and made off with.

NAN  What bogey?

MÍTRITCH  Why, just his very self! (*Climbs up on to the oven.*) The oven is beautifully warm tonight. Quite a treat! Oh Lord! Gracious Nicholas!

NAN  Daddy! are you going to sleep?

MÍTRITCH  What else? Do you think I'm going to sing songs?

(*Silence.*)

NAN     Daddy! Daddy, I say! They are digging! they're digging—don't you hear? Blest if they're not, they're digging!

MÍTRITCH     What are you dreaming about? Digging! Digging in the night! Who's digging? The cow's rubbing herself, that's all. Digging indeed! Go to sleep I tell you, else I'll just put out the light!

NAN     Daddy darling, don't put it out! I won't... truly, truly, I won't. It's so frightful!

MÍTRITCH     Frightful? Don't be afraid and then it won't be frightful. Look at her, she's afraid, and then says it's frightful. How can it help being frightful if you are afraid? Eh, what a stupid little girl!

(*Silence. The cricket chirps.*)

NAN     (*Whispers.*) Daddy! I say, daddy! Are you asleep?

MÍTRITCH     Now then, what d'you want?

NAN     What's the bogey like?

MÍTRITCH     Why, like this! When he finds such a one as you, who won't sleep, he comes with a sack and pops the girl into it, then in he gets himself, head and all, lifts her dress, and gives her a fine whipping!

NAN     What with?

MÍTRITCH     He takes a birch-broom with him.

NAN     But he can't see there—inside the sack!

MÍTRITCH     He'll see, no fear!

NAN  But I'll bite him.

MÍTRITCH  No, friend, him you can't bite!

NAN  Daddy, there's someone coming! Who is it? Oh gracious goodness! Who can it be?

MÍTRITCH  Well, if someone's coming, let them come! What's the matter with you? I suppose it's your mother!

(*Enter* ANÍSYA.)

ANÍSYA  Nan! (NAN *pretends to be asleep.*) Mítritch!

MÍTRITCH  What?

ANÍSYA  What's the lamp burning for? We are going to sleep in the summer-hut.

MÍTRITCH  Why, you see I've only just got straight. I'll put the light out all right.

ANÍSYA  (*Rummages in her box and grumbles.*) When a thing's wanted one never can find it!

MÍTRITCH  Why, what is it you are looking for?

ANÍSYA  I'm looking for a cross. Suppose it were to die unbaptized! It would be a sin, you know!

MÍTRITCH  Of course it would! Everything in due order.... Have you found it?

ANÍSYA  Yes, I've found it. (*Exit.*)

MÍTRITCH  That's right, else I'd have lent her mine. Oh Lord!

NAN  (*Jumps up trembling.*) Oh, oh, daddy! Don't go to sleep; for goodness' sake, don't! It's so frightful!

MÍTRITCH  What's frightful?

NAN     It will die—the little baby will! At Aunt Irene's the old woman also baptized the baby, and it died!

MÍTRITCH     If it dies, they'll bury it!

NAN     But maybe it wouldn't have died, only old Granny Matryóna's there! Didn't I hear what granny was saying? I heard her! Blest if I didn't!

MÍTRITCH     What did you hear? Go to sleep, I tell you. Cover yourself up, head and all, and let's have an end of it!

NAN     If it lived, I'd nurse it!

MÍTRITCH     (*Roars.*) Oh Lord!

NAN     Where will they put it?

MÍTRITCH     In the right place! It's no business of yours! Go to sleep I tell you, else mother will come; she'll give it you! (*Silence.*)

NAN     Daddy! Eh, daddy! That girl, you know, you were telling about—they didn't kill her?

MÍTRITCH     That girl? Oh yes. That girl turned out all right!

NAN     How was it? You were saying you found her?

MÍTRITCH     Well, we just found her!

NAN     But where did you find her? Do tell!

MÍTRITCH     Why, in their own house; that's where! We came to a village, the soldiers began hunting about in the house, when suddenly there's that same little girl lying on the floor, flat on her stomach. We were going to give her a knock on the head, but all at once I felt that sorry, that I took her up in my arms; but no, she wouldn't let me! Made herself so heavy, quite a hundredweight, and caught hold where she could with her hands, so that one couldn't get them off! Well, so I began stroking her head. It was so bristly—just like a hedgehog! So I stroked and stroked, and she quieted down at last. I soaked a bit of rusk and gave it her. She understood that, and began nibbling. What were we to do with her? We took her; took her, and began feeding and feeding her, and she got so used to us that we took her with us on the march, and so she went about with us. Ah, she was a fine girl!

NAN  Yes, and not baptized?

MÍTRITCH  Who can tell! They used to say, not altogether. 'Cos why, those people weren't our own.

NAN  Germans?

MÍTRITCH  What an idea! Germans! Not Germans, but Asiatics. They are just the same as Jews, but still not Jews. Polish, yet Asiatics. Curls... or, Curdlys is their name.... I've forgotten what it is![8] We called the girl Sáshka. She was a fine girl, Sáshka was! There now, I've forgotten everything I used to know! But that girl—the deuce take her—seems to be before my eyes now! Out of all my time of service, I remember how they flogged me, and I remember that girl. That's all I remember! She'd hang round one's neck, and one 'ud carry her so. That was a girl—if you wanted a better you'd not find one! We gave her away afterwards. The captain's wife took her to bring up as her daughter. So—she was all right! How sorry the soldiers were to let her go!

NAN  There now, daddy, and I remember when father was dying—you were not living with us then. Well, he called Nikíta and says, "Forgive me, Nikíta!" he says, and begins to cry. (*Sighs.*) That also felt very sad!

MÍTRITCH  Yes; there now, so it is...

NAN  Daddy! Daddy, I say! There they are again, making a noise in the cellar! Oh gracious heavens! Oh dear! Oh dear! Oh, daddy! They'll do something to it! They'll make away with it, and it's so little! Oh, oh! (*Covers up her head and cries.*)

MÍTRITCH  (*Listening.*) Really they're up to some villainy, blow them to shivers! Oh, these women are vile creatures! One can't say much for men either; but women!... They are like wild beasts, and stick at nothing!

NAN  (*Rising.*) Daddy; I say, daddy!

MÍTRITCH  Well, what now?

NAN  The other day a traveller stayed the night; he said that when an infant died its soul goes up straight to heaven. Is that true?

MÍTRITCH  Who can tell. I suppose so. Well?

NAN    Oh, it would be best if I died too. (*Whimpers.*)

MÍTRITCH    Then you'd be off the list!

NAN    Up to ten one's an infant, and maybe one's soul would go to God. Else one's sure to go to the bad!

MÍTRITCH    And how to the bad? How should the likes of you not go to the bad? Who teaches you? What do you see? What do you hear? Only vileness! I, though I've not been taught much, still know a thing or two. I'm not quite like a peasant woman. A peasant woman, what is she? Just mud! There are many millions of the likes of you in Russia, and all as blind as moles—knowing nothing! All sorts of spells: how to stop the cattle-plague with a plough, and how to cure children by putting them under the perches in the henhouse! That's what they know!

NAN    Yes, mother also did that!

MÍTRITCH    Yes—there it is—just so! So many millions of girls and women, and all like beasts in a forest! As she grows up, so she dies! Never sees anything; never hears anything. A peasant—he may learn something at the pub, or maybe in prison, or in the army—as I did. But a woman? Let alone about God, she doesn't even know rightly what Friday it is! Friday! Friday! But ask her what's Friday? She don't know! They're like blind puppies, creeping about and poking their noses into the dung-heap.... All they

|  |  |
|---|---|
| | know are their silly songs. Ho, ho, ho, ho! But what they mean by ho-ho, they don't know themselves! |
| NAN | But I, daddy, I do know half the Lord's Prayer! |
| MÍTRITCH | A lot you know! But what can one expect of you? Who teaches you? Only a tipsy peasant—with the strap perhaps! That's all the teaching you get! I don't know who'll have to answer for you. For a recruit, the drill-sergeant or the corporal has to answer; but for the likes of you there's no one responsible! Just as the cattle that have no herdsman are the most mischievous, so with you women—you are the stupidest class! The most foolish class is yours! |
| NAN | Then what's one to do? |
| MÍTRITCH | That's what one has to do.... You just cover up your head and sleep! Oh Lord! |
| | (*Silence. The cricket chirps.*) |
| NAN | (*Jumps up.*) Daddy! Someone's screaming awfully! Blest if someone isn't screaming! Daddy darling, it's coming here! |
| MÍTRITCH | Cover up your head, I tell you! |
| | (*Enter* NIKÍTA, *followed by* MATRYÓNA.) |
| NIKÍTA | What have they done with me? What have they done with me? |
| MATRYÓNA | Have a drop, honey; have a drop of drink! What's the matter? (*Fetches the spirits and sets the bottle before him.*) |
| NIKÍTA | Give it here! Perhaps the drink will help me! |

MATRYÓNA  Mind! They're not asleep! Here you are, have a drop!

NIKÍTA  What does it all mean? Why did you plan it? You might have taken it somewhere!

MATRYÓNA  (*Whispers.*) Sit still a bit and drink a little more, or have a smoke. It will ease your thoughts!

NIKÍTA  My own mother! My turn seems to have come! How it began to whimper, and how the little bones crunched... krr... I'm not a man now!

MATRYÓNA  Eh, now, what's the use of talking so silly! Of course it does seem fearsome at night, but wait till the daylight comes, and a day or two passes, and you'll forget to think of it! (*Goes up to* NIKÍTA *and puts her hand on his shoulder.*)

NIKÍTA  Go away from me! What have you done with me?

MATRYÓNA  Come, come, sonnie! Now really, what's the matter with you? (*Takes his hand.*)

NIKÍTA  Go away from me! I'll kill you! It's all one to me now! I'll kill you!

MATRYÓNA  Oh, oh, how frightened he's got! You should go and have a sleep now!

NIKÍTA  I have nowhere to go; I'm lost!

MATRYÓNA  (*Shaking her head.*) Oh, oh, I'd better go and tidy things up. He'll sit and rest a bit, and it will pass! (*Exit.*)

(NIKÍTA *sits with his face in his hands.* MÍTRITCH *and* NAN *seem stunned.*)

NIKÍTA  It's whining! It's whining! It is really—there,

|   |   |
|---|---|
| | there, quite plain! She'll bury it, really she will! (*Runs to the door.*) Mother, don't bury it, it's alive.... |
| | (*Enter* MATRYÓNA.) |
| MATRYÓNA | (*Whispers.*) Now then, what is it? Heaven help you! Why won't you get to rest? How can it be alive? All its bones are crushed! |
| NIKÍTA | Give me more drink! (*Drinks.*) |
| MATRYÓNA | Now go, sonnie. You'll fall asleep now all right. |
| NIKÍTA | (*Stands listening.*) Still alive... there... it's whining! Don't you hear?... There! |
| MATRYÓNA | (*Whispers.*) No! I tell you! |
| NIKÍTA | Mother! My own mother! I've ruined my life! What have you done with me? Where am I to go? (*Runs out of the hut;* MATRYÓNA *follows him.*) |
| NAN | Daddy dear, darling, they've smothered it! |
| MÍTRITCH | (*Angrily.*) Go to sleep, I tell you! Oh dear, may the frogs kick you! I'll give it to you with the broom! Go to sleep, I tell you! |
| NAN | Daddy, my treasure! Something is catching hold of my shoulders, something is catching hold with its paws! Daddy dear... really, really... I must go! Daddy, darling! let me get up on the oven with you! Let me, for Heaven's sake! Catching hold... catching hold! Oh! (*Runs to the stove.*) |
| MÍTRITCH | See how they've frightened the girl.... What vile creatures they are! May the frogs kick |

them! Well then, climb up.

NAN (*Climbs on oven.*) But don't you go away!

MÍTRITCH Where should I go to? Climb up, climb up! Oh Lord! Gracious Nicholas! Holy Mother!... How they have frighted the girl. (*Covers her up.*) There's a little fool—really a little fool! How they've frighted her; really, they are vile creatures! The deuce take 'em!

(*Curtain.*)

# Act V

## Scene I

In front of scene a stack-stand, to the left a thrashing ground, to the right a barn. The barn doors are open. Straw is strewn about in the doorway. The hut with yard and outbuildings is seen in the background, whence proceed sounds of singing and of a tambourine. Two GIRLS are walking past the barn towards the hut.

FIRST GIRL  There, you see we've managed to pass without so much as getting our boots dirty! But to come by the street is terribly muddy! (*Stop and wipe their boots on the straw.* FIRST GIRL *looks at the straw and sees something.*) What's that?

SECOND GIRL  (*Looks where the straw lies and sees someone.*) It's Mítritch, their labourer. Just look how drunk he is!

FIRST GIRL  Why, I thought he didn't drink.

SECOND GIRL  It seems he didn't, until it was going around.

FIRST GIRL  Just see! He must have come to fetch some straw. Look! he's got a rope in his hand, and he's fallen asleep.

SECOND GIRL  (*Listening.*) They're still singing the praises.[9] So I s'pose the bride and bridegroom have not yet been blessed! They say Akoulína didn't even lament![10]

| | |
|---|---|
| FIRST GIRL | Mammie says she is marrying against her will. Her stepfather threatened her, or else she'd not have done it for the world! Why, you know what they've been saying about her? |
| MARÍNA | (*Catching up the* GIRLS.) How d'you do, lassies? |
| GIRLS | How d'you do? |
| MARÍNA | Going to the wedding, my dears? |
| FIRST GIRL | It's nearly over! We've come just to have a look. |
| MARÍNA | Would you call my old man for me? Simon, from Zoúevo; but surely you know him? |
| FIRST GIRL | To be sure we do; he's a relative of the bridegroom's, I think? |
| MARÍNA | Of course; he's my old man's nephew, the bridegroom is. |
| SECOND GIRL | Why don't you go yourself? Fancy not going to a wedding! |
| MARÍNA | I have no mind for it, and no time either. It's time for us to be going home. We didn't mean to come to the wedding. We were taking oats to town. We only stopped to feed the horse, and they made my old man go in. |
| FIRST GIRL | Where did you put up then? At Fyódoritch's? |
| MARÍNA | Yes. Well then, I'll stay here and you go and call him, my dear—my old man. Call him, my pet, and say "Your missis, Marína, says you must go now!" His mates are harnessing. |
| FIRST GIRL | Well, all right—if you won't go in yourself. |

(*The* GIRLS *go away towards the house along a*

*footpath. Sounds of songs and tambourine.*)

MARÍNA (*Alone, stands thinking.*) I might go in, but I don't like to, because I have not met him since that day he threw me over. It's more than a year now. But I'd have liked to have a peep and see how he lives with his Anísya. People say they don't get on. She's a coarse woman, and with a character of her own. I should think he's remembered me more than once. He's been caught by the idea of a comfortable life and has changed me for it. But, God help him, I don't cherish ill-will! Then it hurt! Oh dear, it was pain! But now it's worn away and been forgotten. But I'd like to have seen him. (*Looks towards hut and sees* NIKÍTA.) Look there! Why, he is coming here! Have the girls told him? How's it he has left his guests? I'll go away! (NIKÍTA *approaches, hanging his head down, swinging his arms, and muttering.*) And how sullen he looks!

NIKÍTA (*Sees and recognises* MARÍNA.) Marína, dearest friend, little Marína, what do you want?

MARÍNA I have come for my old man.

NIKÍTA Why didn't you come to the wedding? You might have had a look round, and a laugh at my expense!

MARÍNA What have I to laugh at? I've come for my husband.

NIKÍTA Ah, Marína dear! (*Tries to embrace her.*)

MARÍNA (*Steps angrily aside.*) You'd better drop that sort

of thing, Nikíta! What has been, is past! I've come for my husband. Is he in your house?

NIKÍTA   So I must not remember the past? You won't let me?

MARÍNA   It's no use recalling the past! What used to be is over now!

NIKÍTA   And can never come back, you mean?

MARÍNA   And will never come back! But why have you gone away? You, the master—and to go away from the feast!

NIKÍTA   (*Sits down on the straw.*) Why have I gone away? Eh, if you knew, if you had any idea... I'm dull, Marína, so dull that I wish my eyes would not see! I rose from the table and left them, to get away from the people. If I could only avoid seeing anyone!

MARÍNA   (*Coming nearer to him.*) How's that?

NIKÍTA   This is how it is: when I eat, it's there! When I drink, it's there! When I sleep, it's there! I'm so sick of it—so sick! But it's chiefly because I'm all alone that I'm so sick, little Marína. I have no one to share my trouble.

MARÍNA   You can't live your life without trouble, Nikíta. However, I've wept over mine and wept it away.

NIKÍTA   The former, the old trouble! Ah, dear friend, you've wept yours away, and I've got mine up to there! (*Puts his hand to his throat.*)

MARÍNA   But why?

NIKÍTA   Why, I'm sick of my whole life! I am sick of myself! Ah, Marína, why did you not know how to keep me? You've ruined me, and yourself too! Is this life?

MARÍNA   (*Stands by the barn crying, but restrains herself.*) I do not complain of my life, Nikíta! God grant everyone a life like mine. I do not complain. I confessed to my old man at the time, and he forgave me. And he does not reproach me. I'm not discontented with my life. The old man is quiet, and is fond of me, and I keep his children clothed and washed! He is really kind to me. Why should I complain? It seems God willed it so. And what's the matter with your life? You are rich...

NIKÍTA   My life!... It's only that I don't wish to disturb the wedding feast, or I'd take this rope here (*takes hold of the rope on the straw*) and throw it across that rafter there. Then I'd make a noose and stretch it out, and I'd climb on to that rafter and jump down with my head in the noose! That's what my life is!

MARÍNA   That's enough! Lord help you!

NIKÍTA   You think I'm joking? You think I'm drunk? I'm not drunk! Today even drink takes no hold on me! I'm devoured by misery! Misery is eating me up completely, so that I care for nothing! Oh, little Marína, it's only with you I ever lived! Do you remember how we used to while away the nights together at the railway?

MARÍNA  Don't you rub the sores, Nikíta! I'm bound legally now, and you too. My sin has been forgiven, don't disturb...

NIKÍTA  What shall I do with my heart? Where am I to turn to?

MARÍNA  What's there to be done? You've got a wife. Don't go looking at others, but keep to your own! You loved Anísya, then go on loving her!

NIKÍTA  Oh, that Anísya, she's gall and wormwood to me, but she's round my feet like rank weeds!

MARÍNA  Whatever she is, still she's your wife.... But what's the use of talking; you'd better go to your visitors, and send my husband to me.

NIKÍTA  Oh dear, if you knew the whole business... but there's no good talking!

(*Enter* MARÍNA'S HUSBAND, *red and tipsy, and* NAN.)

MARÍNA'S HUSBAND  Marína! Missis! My old woman! are you here?

NIKÍTA  There's your husband calling you. Go!

MARÍNA  And you?

NIKÍTA  I? I'll lie down here for a bit! (*Lies down on the straw.*)

HUSBAND  Where is she then?

NAN  There she is, near the barn.

HUSBAND  What are you standing there for? Come to the feast! The hosts want you to come and do them honour! The wedding party is just going to start, and then we can go too.

MARÍNA  (*Going towards her husband.*) I didn't want to go in.

HUSBAND  Come on, I tell you! You'll drink a glass to our nephew Peter's health, the rascal! Else the hosts might take offence! There's plenty of time for our business. (MARÍNA'S HUSBAND *puts his arm around her, and goes reeling out with her.*)

NIKÍTA  (*Rises and sits down on the straw.*) Ah, now that I've seen her, life seems more sickening than ever! It was only with her that I ever really lived! I've ruined my life for nothing! I've done for myself! (*Lies down.*) Where can I go? If mother earth would but open and swallow me!

NAN  (*Sees* NIKÍTA, *and runs towards him.*) Daddy, I say, daddy! They're looking for you! Her godfather and all of them have already blessed her. Truly they have, they're getting cross!

NIKÍTA  (*Aside.*) Where can I go to?

NAN  What? What are you saying?

NIKÍTA  I'm not saying anything! Don't bother!

NAN  Daddy! Come, I say! (NIKÍTA *is silent,* NAN *pulls him by the hand.*) Dad, go and bless them! My word, they're angry, they're grumbling!

NIKÍTA  (*Drags away his hand.*) Leave me alone!

NAN  Now then!

NIKÍTA  (*Threatens her with the rope.*) Go, I say! I'll give it you!

NAN  Then I'll send mother! (*Runs away.*)

NIKÍTA  (*Rises.*) How can I go? How can I take the holy icon in my hands? How am I to look her in the face! (*Lies down again.*) Oh, if there were a hole in the ground, I'd jump in! No one should see me, and I should see no one! (*Rises again.*) No, I shan't go... May they all go to the devil, I shan't go! (*Takes the rope and makes a noose, and tries it on his neck.*) That's the way!

(*Enter* MATRYÓNA. NIKÍTA *sees his mother, takes the rope off his neck, and again lies down in the straw.*)

MATRYÓNA  (*Comes in hurriedly.*) Nikíta! Nikíta, I say! He don't even answer! Nikíta, what's the matter? Have you had a drop too much? Come, Nikíta dear; come, honey! The people are tired of waiting.

NIKÍTA  Oh dear, what have you done with me? I'm a lost man!

MATRYÓNA  But what is the matter then? Come, my own; come, give them your blessing, as is proper and honourable, and then it'll all be over! Why, the people are waiting!

NIKÍTA  How can I give blessings?

MATRYÓNA  Why, in the usual way! Don't you know?

NIKÍTA  I know, I know! But who is it I am to bless? What have I done to her?

MATRYÓNA  What have you done? Eh, now he's going to remember it! Why, who knows anything about it? Not a soul! And the girl is going of her own accord.

NIKÍTA  Yes, but how?

MATRYÓNA  Because she's afraid, of course. But still she's going. Besides, what's to be done now? She should have thought sooner! Now she can't refuse. And his kinsfolk can't take offence either. They saw the girl twice, and get money with her too! It's all safe and sound!

NIKÍTA  Yes, but what's in the cellar?

MATRYÓNA  (*Laughs.*) In the cellar? Why, cabbages, mushrooms, potatoes, I suppose! Why remember the past?

NIKÍTA  I'd be only too glad to forget it; but I can't! When I let my mind go, it's just as if I heard.... Oh, what have you done with me?

MATRYÓNA  Now, what are you humbugging for?

NIKÍTA  (*Turns face downward.*) Mother! Don't torment me! I've got it up to there! (*Puts his hand to his throat.*)

MATRYÓNA  Still it has to be done! As it is, people are talking. "The master's gone away and won't come; he can't make up his mind to give his blessing." They'll be putting two and two together. As soon as they see you're frightened they'll begin guessing. "The thief none suspect who walks bold and erect!" But you'll be getting out of the frying-pan into the fire!

|           | Above all, lad, don't show it; don't lose courage, else they'll find out all the more! |
|-----------|---|
| NIKÍTA    | Oh dear! You have snared me into a trap! |
| MATRYÓNA  | That'll do, I tell you; come along! Come in and give your blessing, as is right and honourable;—and there's an end of the matter! |
| NIKÍTA    | (*Lies face down.*) I can't! |
| MATRYÓNA  | (*Aside.*) What has come over him? He seemed all right, and suddenly this comes over him! It seems he's bewitched! Get up, Nikíta! See! There's Anísya coming; she's left her guests! |

(ANÍSYA *enters, dressed up, red and tipsy.*)

| ANÍSYA    | Oh, how nice it is, mother! So nice, so respectable! And how the people are pleased.... But where is he? |
|-----------|---|
| MATRYÓNA  | Here, honey, he's here; he's laid down on the straw and there he lies! He won't come! |
| NIKÍTA    | (*Looking at his wife.*) Just see, she's tipsy too! When I look at her my heart seems to turn! How can one live with her? (*Turns on his face.*) I'll kill her some day! It'll be worse then! |
| ANÍSYA    | Only look, how he's got all among the straw! Is it the drink? (*Laughs.*) I'd not mind lying down there with you, but I've no time! Come, I'll lead you! It is so nice in the house! It's a treat to look on! A concertina! And the women singing so well! All tipsy! Everything so respectable, so nice! |
| NIKÍTA    | What's nice? |

ANÍSYA   The wedding—such a jolly wedding! They all say it's quite an uncommon fine wedding! All so respectable, so nice! Come along! We'll go together! I have had a drop, but I can give you a hand yet! (*Takes his hand.*)

NIKÍTA   (*Pulls it back with disgust.*) Go alone! I'll come!

ANÍSYA   What are you humbugging for? We've got rid of all the bother, we've got rid of her as came between us; now we have nothing to do but to live and be merry! And all so respectable, and quite legal! I'm so pleased! I have no words for it! It's just as if I were going to marry you over again! And oh, the people, they *are* pleased! They're all thanking us! And the guests are all of the best: Iván Moséitch is there, and the Police Officer; they've also been singing songs of praise!

NIKÍTA   Then you should have stayed with them! What have you come for?

ANÍSYA   True enough, I must go back! Else what does it look like! The hosts both go and leave the visitors! And the guests are all of the best!

NIKÍTA   (*Gets up and brushes the straw off himself.*) Go, and I'll come at once!

MATRYÓNA   Just see! He listens to the young bird, but wouldn't listen to the old one! He would not hear me, but he follows his wife at once! (MATRYÓNA *and* ANÍSYA *turn to go.*) Well, are you coming?

NIKÍTA   I'll come directly! You go and I'll follow! I'll

come and give my blessing! (*The women stop.*) Go on! I'll follow! Now then, go! (*Exit women. Sits down and takes his boots off.*) Yes, I'm going! A likely thing! No, you'd better look at the rafter for me! I'll fix the noose and jump with it from the rafter, then you can look for me! And the rope is here just handy. (*Ponders.*) I'd have got over it, over any sorrow—I'd have got over that. But this now—here it is, deep in my heart, and I can't get over it! (*Looks towards the yard.*) Surely she's not coming back? (*Imitates* ANÍSYA.) "So nice, so nice. I'd lie down here with you." Oh, the baggage! Well then, here I am! Come and cuddle when they've taken me down from the rafter! There's only one way! (*Takes the rope and pulls it.*)

(MÍTRITCH, *who is tipsy, sits up and won't let go of the rope.*)

MÍTRITCH    Shan't give it up! Shan't give it to no one! I'll bring it myself! I said I'd bring the straw—and so I will! Nikíta, is that you? (*Laughs.*) Oh, the devil! Have you come to get the straw?

NIKÍTA    Give me the rope!

MÍTRITCH    No, you wait a bit! The peasants sent me! I'll bring it... (*Rises to his feet and begins getting the straw together, but reels for a time, then falls.*) It has beaten me. It's stronger...

NIKÍTA    Give me the rope!

MÍTRITCH    Didn't I say I won't! Oh, Nikíta, you're as stupid as a hog! (*Laughs.*) I love you, but you're a fool! You see that I'm drunk... devil take you! You think I need you?... You just look at me; I'm a Non... fool, can't say it—Noncommissioned Officer of Her Majesty's very First Regiment of Grenadier Guards! I've served Tsar and country, loyal and true! But who am I? You think I'm a warrior? No, I'm not a warrior; I'm the very least of men, a poor lost orphan! I swore not to drink, and now I had a smoke, and... Well then, do you think I'm afraid of you? No fear; I'm afraid of no man! I've taken to drink, and I'll drink! Now I'll go it for a fortnight; I'll go it hard! I'll drink my last shirt; I'll drink my cap; I'll pawn my passport; and I'm afraid of no one! They flogged me in the army to stop me drinking! They switched and switched! "Well," they say, "will you leave off?" "No," says I! Why should I be afraid of them? Here I am! Such as I am, God made me! I swore off drinking, and didn't drink. Now I've took to drink, and I'll drink! And I fear no man! 'Cos I don't lie; but just as... Why should one mind them—such muck as they are! "Here you are," I say; that's me. A priest told me, the devil's the biggest bragger! "As soon," says he, "as you begin to brag, you get frightened; and as soon as you fear men, then the hoofed one just collars you and pushes you where he likes!" But as I don't fear men, I'm easy! I can spit in the devil's beard, and at the sow his mother! He can't do me no harm! There, put that in your pipe!

NIKÍTA (*Crossing himself.*) True enough! What was I about? (*Throws down the rope.*)

MÍTRITCH What?

NIKÍTA (*Rises.*) You tell me not to fear men?

MÍTRITCH Why fear such muck as they are? You look at 'em in the bathhouse! All made of one paste! One has a bigger belly, another a smaller; that's all the difference there is! Fancy being afraid of 'em! Deuce take 'em!

NIKÍTA True enough! What was I about?

MÍTRITCH What?

NIKÍTA You tell me not to fear men?

MÍTRITCH Why fear such muck as they are? You look at 'em in the bathhouse!

MATRYÓNA (*From the yard.*) Well, are you coming?

NIKÍTA Ah! Better so! I'm coming! (*Goes towards yard.*)

## Scene II

Interior of hut, full of people, some sitting round tables and others standing. In the front corner AKOULÍNA and the BRIDEGROOM. On one of the tables an Icon and a loaf of rye-bread. Among the visitors are MARÍNA, her HUSBAND, and a POLICE OFFICER, also a HIRED DRIVER, the MATCHMAKER, and the BEST MAN. The women are singing. ANÍSYA carries round the drink. The singing stops.

| | |
|---|---|
| THE DRIVER | If we are to go, let's go! The church ain't so near. |
| THE BEST MAN | All right; you wait a bit till the stepfather has given his blessing. But where is he? |
| ANÍSYA | He is coming—coming at once, dear friends! Have another glass all of you; don't refuse! |
| THE MATCHMAKER | Why is he so long? We've been waiting such a time! |
| ANÍSYA | He's coming; coming directly, coming in no time! He'll be here before one could plait a girl's hair who's had her hair cropped! Drink, friends! (*Offers the drink.*) Coming at once! Sing again, my pets, meanwhile! |
| THE DRIVER | They've sung all their songs, waiting here! |

(*The women sing.* NIKÍTA *and* AKÍM *enter during the singing.*)

| | |
|---|---|
| NIKÍTA | (*Holds his father's arm and pushes him in before him.*) Go, father; I can't do without you! |
| AKÍM | I don't like—I mean what d'ye call it... |
| NIKÍTA | (*To the women.*) Enough! Be quiet! (*Looks round the hut.*) Marína, are you there? |
| THE MATCHMAKER | Go, take the icon, and give them your blessing! |
| NIKÍTA | Wait a while! (*Looks round.*) Akoulína, are you there? |
| MATCHMAKER | What are you calling everybody for? Where should she be? How queer he seems! |

126

ANÍSYA   Gracious goodness! Why, he's barefoot!

NIKÍTA   Father, you are here! Look at me! Christian Commune, you are all here, and I am here! I am... (*Falls on his knees.*)

ANÍSYA   Nikíta darling, what's the matter with you? Oh my head, my head!

MATCHMAKER   Here's a go!

MATRYÓNA   I did say he was taking too much of that French wine! Come to your senses; what are you about?

(*They try to lift him; he takes no heed of them, but looks in front of him.*)

NIKÍTA   Christian Commune! I have sinned, and I wish to confess!

MATRYÓNA   (*Shakes him by the shoulder.*) Are you mad? Dear friends, he's gone crazy! He must be taken away!

NIKÍTA   (*Shakes her off.*) Leave me alone! And you, father, hear me! And first, Marína, look here! (*Bows to the ground to her and rises.*) I have sinned towards you! I promised to marry you, I tempted you, and forsook you! Forgive me, in Christ's name! (*Again bows to the ground before her.*)

ANÍSYA   And what are you drivelling about? It's not becoming! No one wants to know! Get up! It's like your impudence!

MATRYÓNA   Oh, oh, he's bewitched! And however did it happen? It's a spell! Get up! what nonsense

|   |   |
|---|---|
| | are you jabbering? (*Pulls him.*) |
| NIKÍTA | (*Shakes his head.*) Don't touch me! Forgive me my sin towards you, Marína! Forgive me, for Christ's sake! |

(MARÍNA *covers her face with her hands in silence.*)

|   |   |
|---|---|
| ANÍSYA | Get up, I tell you! Don't be so impudent! What are you thinking about—to recall it? Enough humbug! It's shameful! Oh my poor head! He's quite crazy! |
| NIKÍTA | (*Pushes his wife away and turns to* AKOULÍNA.) Akoulína, now I'll speak to you! Listen, Christian Commune! I'm a fiend, Akoulína! I have sinned against you! Your father died no natural death! He was poisoned! |
| ANÍSYA | (*Screams.*) Oh my head! What's he about? |
| MATRYÓNA | The man's beside himself! Lead him away! |

(*The folk come up and try to seize him.*)

|   |   |
|---|---|
| AKÍM | (*Motions them back with his arms.*) Wait! You lads, what d'ye call it, wait, I mean! |
| NIKÍTA | Akoulína, I poisoned him! Forgive me, in Christ's name! |
| AKOULÍNA | (*Jumps up.*) He's telling lies! I know who did it! |
| MATCHMAKER | What are you about? You sit still! |
| AKÍM | Oh Lord, what sins, what sins! |
| POLICE | Seize him, and send for the Elder! We must |

OFFICER    draw up an indictment and have witnesses to it! Get up and come here!

AKÍM    (*To* POLICE OFFICER.) Now you—with the bright buttons—I mean, you wait! Let him, what d'ye call it, speak out, I mean!

POLICE OFFICER    Mind, old man, and don't interfere! I have to draw up an indictment!

AKÍM    Eh, what a fellow you are; wait, I say! Don't talk, I mean, about, what d'ye call it, 'ditements! Here God's work is being done.... A man is confessing, I mean! And you, what d'ye call it... 'ditements!

POLICE OFFICER    The Elder!

AKÍM    Let God's work be done, I mean, and then you, I mean, you do your business!

NIKÍTA    And, Akoulína, my sin is great towards you; I seduced you; forgive me in Christ's name! (*Bows to the ground before her.*)

AKOULÍNA    (*Leaves the table.*) Let me go! I shan't be married! He told me to, but I shan't now!

POLICE OFFICER    Repeat what you have said.

NIKÍTA    Wait, sir, let me finish!

AKÍM    (*With rapture.*) Speak, my son! Tell everything—you'll feel better! Confess to God, don't fear men! God—God! It is He!

NIKÍTA    I poisoned the father, dog that I am, and I ruined the daughter! She was in my power,

|              |                                                                                                                                                                                                                                                                                                                     |
| ------------ | ------------------------------------------------------------------------------------------------------------------------------------------------------------------------------------------------------------------------------------------------------------------------------------------------------------------- |
|              | and I ruined her, and her baby!                                                                                                                                                                                                                                                                                     |
| AKOULÍNA     | True, that's true!                                                                                                                                                                                                                                                                                                  |
| NIKÍTA       | I smothered the baby in the cellar with a board! I sat on it and smothered it—and its bones crunched! (*Weeps.*) And I buried it! I did it, all alone!                                                                                                                                                              |
| AKOULÍNA     | He raves! I told him to!                                                                                                                                                                                                                                                                                            |
| NIKÍTA       | Don't shield me! I fear no one now! Forgive me, Christian Commune! (*Bows to the ground.*)                                                                                                                                                                                                                          |
|              | (*Silence.*)                                                                                                                                                                                                                                                                                                        |
| POLICE OFFICER | Bind him! The marriage is evidently off!                                                                                                                                                                                                                                                                          |
|              | (*Men come up with their belts.*)                                                                                                                                                                                                                                                                                   |
| NIKÍTA       | Wait, there's plenty of time! (*Bows to the ground before his father.*) Father, dear father, forgive me too—fiend that I am! You told me from the first, when I took to bad ways, you said then, "If a claw is caught, the bird is lost!" I would not listen to your words, dog that I was, and it has turned out as you said! Forgive me, for Christ's sake! |
| AKÍM         | (*Rapturously.*) God will forgive you, my own son! (*Embraces him.*) You have had no mercy on yourself, He will show mercy on you! God—God! It is He!                                                                                                                                                               |
|              | (*Enter* ELDER.)                                                                                                                                                                                                                                                                                                    |
| ELDER        | There are witnesses enough here.                                                                                                                                                                                                                                                                                    |
| POLICE       | We will have the examination at once.                                                                                                                                                                                                                                                                               |

OFFICER

          (NIKÍTA *is bound.*)

AKOULÍNA  (*Goes and stands by his side.*) I shall tell the truth! Ask me!

NIKÍTA  (*Bound.*) No need to ask! I did it all myself. The design was mine, and the deed was mine. Take me where you like. I will say no more!

(*Curtain.*)

# Endnotes

1. It is customary to place a dying person under the icon. One or more icons hang in the hut of each Orthodox peasant. ↵
2. Peasant weddings are usually in autumn. They are forbidden in Lent, and soon after Easter the peasants become too busy to marry till harvest is over. ↵
3. A formal request for forgiveness is customary among Russians, but it is often no mere formality. Nikíta's first reply is evasive; his second reply, "God will forgive you," is the correct one sanctioned by custom. ↵
4. Loud public wailing of this kind is customary, and considered indispensable, among the peasants. ↵
5. Where not otherwise mentioned in the stage directions, it is always the winter half of the hut that is referred to as "the hut." The summer half is not heated, and not used in winter under ordinary circumstances. ↵
6. The Foundlings' Hospital in Moscow, where eighty to ninety percent of the children die. ↵
7. Nan calls Mítritch "daddy" merely as a term of endearment. ↵
8. Probably Kurds. ↵
9. This refers to the songs customary at the wedding of Russian peasants, praising the bride and bridegroom. ↵
10. It is etiquette for a bride to bewail the approaching loss of her maidenhood. ↵

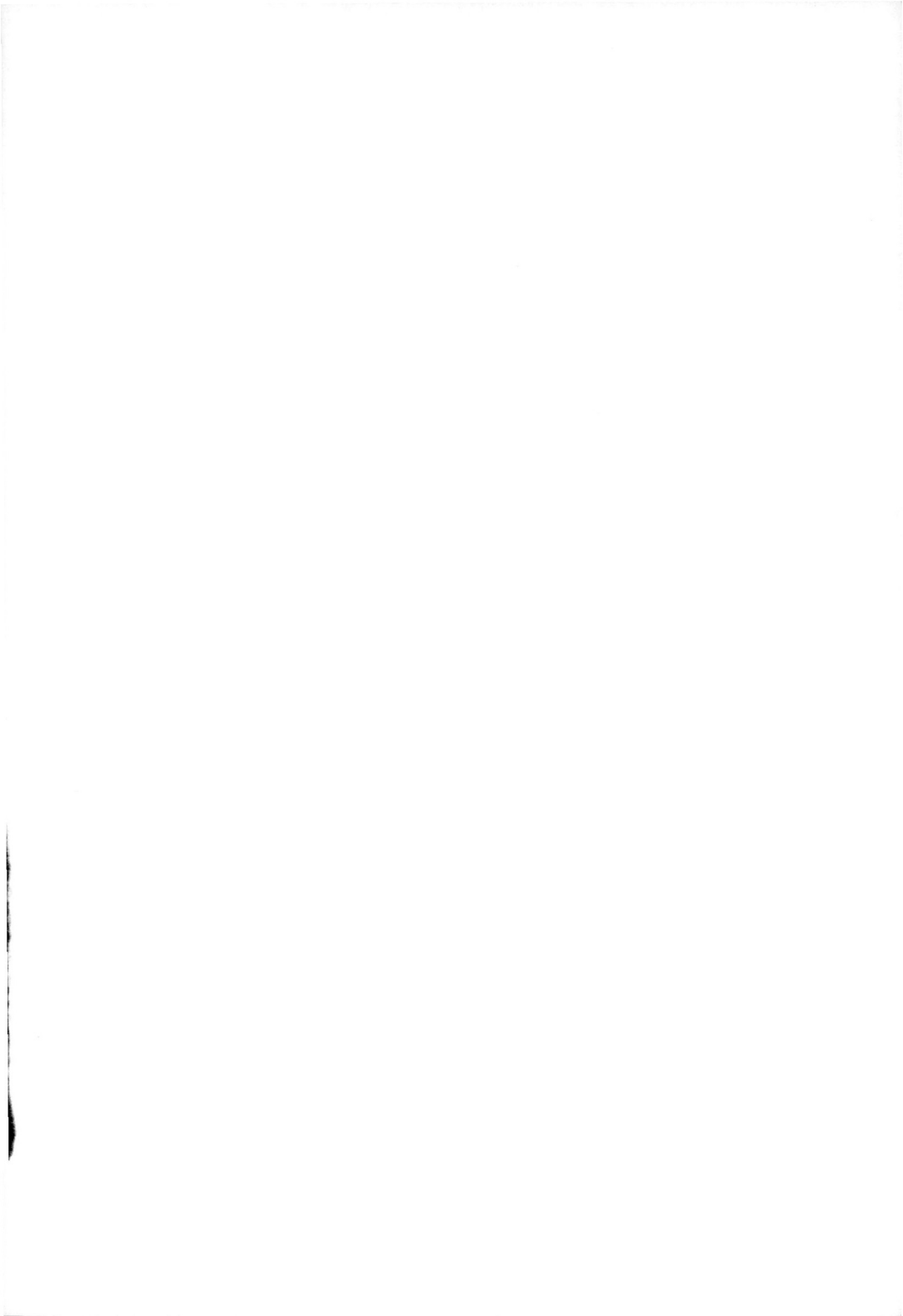